# The Divine Redemption

Billy Henrickle, Mark Mayeux

Copyright © 2025 by Billy Henrickle, Mark Mayeux

All rights reserved.

No part of this publication may be reproduced, distributed, or transmitted in any form or by any means, including photocopying, recording, or other electronic or mechanical methods, without the prior written permission of the publisher, except as permitted by U.S. copyright law.

The story, all names, characters, and incidents portrayed in this production are fictitious. No identification with actual persons (living or deceased), places, buildings, and products is intended or should be inferred.

This book is not meant to offend or discredit any race or religion whatsoever and is strictly for entertainment purposes only.

Published by Main Street Digital Agency

Book Cover & Formatting by Mindy Fruhmann

First Edition

MARK 9:43  And if your hand causes you to sin, cut it off. It is better for you to enter life maimed or crippled, then with two hands to go into Gehenna, to the unquenchable fire.

# Contents

| | |
|---|---|
| CHAPTER 1: THE PHANTOM OF ORLEANS | 1 |
| CHAPTER 2: HIS REIGN AND REPUTATION GROWS | 23 |
| CHAPTER 3: DEVILISH DEACON? | 40 |
| CHAPTER 4: REACQUAINTANCE | 56 |
| CHAPTER 5: FORGIVE ME FATHER, FOR I HAVE SINNED | 70 |
| CHAPTER 6: A FAMILIAR FACE | 86 |
| CHAPTER 7: SPEAK NO EVIL | 93 |
| CHAPTER 8: BLASPHEMOUS TONGUE | 106 |
| CHAPTER 9: POLICY OF PUNISHMENT | 118 |
| CHAPTER 10: THE NET CLOSES IN | 135 |
| CHAPTER 11: AFTERMATH | 157 |

# CHAPTER 1: THE PHANTOM OF ORLEANS

It was late into the night, and light rain fell softly over the vibrant streets of New Orleans. On Bourbon Street, the very heartbeat of this rowdy city, life pulsed with an energy that was both intoxicating and chaotic. Neon lights illuminated the thoroughfare in a dazzling array of colors, casting vivid reflections on the wet pavement below. The air was thick with the mingling scents of humidity and alcohol, a potent combination that enveloped everyone in its embrace.

Inside Rick's Cabaret, known as the premier gentleman's club of New Orleans, the atmosphere was just as electrifying. The music blared loudly, an electric mix of upbeat tunes that filled the air with a contagious rhythm. Dancers moved energetically across the stage, their bodies twisting and turning in mesmerizing displays, captivating the eyes of the crowd. The patrons, a mix of locals and excited tourists, reveled in the debauchery that surrounded them, each lost in their own world of indulgence.

Among them was a particularly disheveled man, his appearance marked by the remnants of a night spent indulging in top-shelf liquor and countless VIP lap dances. His eyes were glazed over, reflecting the vibrant lights but devoid of clarity. It was late, he had spent his allotted money, plus he was a bit drunk. The man stumbled out of the popular club, the world around him swaying as if caught in the rhythm of the music still echoing in his mind. The rain kissed his face, the cool droplets mixing with the warmth of the alcohol that coursed through his veins, adding to the surrealness of the moment. As he made his way through the rain-slicked streets, his movements unsteady, a shadowy figure observed him from a distance. Cloaked in darkness, the figure moved with a silent grace, each step deliberate and fluid, reminiscent of a cat stalking its prey. The anonymity of the shadow lent an air of mystery to the scene, the figure's face partially obscured, evoking an unsettling feeling.

As the drunken man navigated the neon-soaked streets, the shadowy figure began to follow him, slipping through the shadows as easily as smoke dispersing in the air. The contrast between the revelry of Bourbon Street and the ominous presence that trailed behind him created a profound tension. He turned down a side street, oblivious to the threat lurking not far behind him.

A block or two later, he entered a semi-deserted parking garage, the sound of rain pattering against the concrete, the only thing breaking the silence. It was here that the figure caught up with him, emerging from the shadows with an unsettling calmness. The dim lighting of the garage cast eerie shapes across the walls, making it difficult to discern friend from foe. The once lively atmosphere of Bourbon Street felt worlds away, replaced by the stark reality of this quiet, hidden space.

## CHAPTER 1: THE PHANTOM OF ORLEANS

With the rain continuing to fall outside, the garage became a shelter of secrets, where intentions remained shrouded in darkness. As the drunken man leaned against a cold concrete pillar, trying to regain his bearings, he had no idea of the impending confrontation about to unfold. The night was far from over, and in the depths of New Orleans, the stories continued to twist and turn, drawing all who wandered into its mysterious embrace.

The city continued to hum with the energy of a late-night revelry. Streetlights cast a warm glow on the bustling crowds, their laughter and chatter mingling with the distant rumble of traffic. Yet, in this shadowed alleyway, a different kind of drama was unfolding. A drunken man, impervious to the impending danger, relieved himself against a parked car, his figure silhouetted against the dim light. His guard was down, his senses dulled by the intoxicating liquid and urine passing out of his system.

Suddenly, the cloaked figure emerged from the darkness. His eyes, glinting with a sinister intensity, pierced the night. A chill wind swept through the alleyway, stirring the man's numbed senses. But it was too late. With a swift, precise movement, the attacker lunged forward. A sharp blade flashed in the dim light, slicing through the man's right eye. A blood-curdling scream echoed through the alley, penetrating the festive noise of the city. Pain, searing and intense, consumed the helpless victim.

"I have been entrusted by him with immense responsibilities," the attacker hissed, his voice cold and menacing. "I will save you from Gehenna." Another strike followed, more brutal than the first. The blade again descended, severing what remained of the man's eye. The victim could hear the crunching of the blade as the attacker dug his eyeball from its socket. He was left blind, his vision replaced by a crimson haze and then darkness. The attacker, his mission complete, vanished into the night, disappearing into the naive crowd. The wounded victim, bloodied and disoriented, was left alone. His screams for help were swallowed by the city's cacophony. Yet, amidst the chaos, a flicker of hope remained. Despite the shock and immense pain, he managed to reach for his phone, his trembling fingers dialing 911.

He laid out sprawled on the cold, damp concrete, a stark contrast to the hot vibrant life that throbbed through the city streets. His face, a canvas of violence, was marred by a deep, crimson wound. Blood, thick and viscous, pooled around his head, staining the once pristine concrete. His eyes, once filled with life, were now blank and distant, a vacant stare fixed upon the indifferent sky. The festive lights, which had once cast a warm glow upon him and the city, now seemed to mock the horror that had unfolded in the darkness. The joyous laughter and lively music that had filled the air were replaced by an eerie silence, broken only by the distant wail of sirens.

The attacker, a phantom in the night, had vanished without a trace. His identity, a mystery shrouded in darkness, remained a haunting enigma. Emerging from the shadows, a silent specter, his presence felt but not seen. With a swift and brutal efficiency, he had carried out his gruesome deed, leaving behind a trail of blood and fear. And then, as suddenly as he had appeared, this phantom had retreated back into the night, disappearing into the labyrinth of alleyways and darkened streets. The motives or reasons for such a heinous act were lost to the evening, leaving behind a chilling void of uncertainty.

The city, usually filled with petty crimes, was jolted awake once again by the piercing wail of sirens. A dark cloud descended upon the festive atmosphere as news of the brutal attack spread quick-

## CHAPTER 1: THE PHANTOM OF ORLEANS

ly. Emergency services, their vehicles flashing red and blue, raced towards the scene, their urgency palpable. The victim, a symbol of vulnerability, lay injured and alone, a stark reminder of the darkness that lurked beneath the city's vibrant facade. As the numerous onlookers grappled with the horrifying incident, a sense of unease settled in. The realization that evil could thrive, even in the most unexpected places, sent a shiver of uncertainty through its inhabitants and visitors. The once carefree city was now forced to confront its sinister side, a stark reminder of the fragility of safety and the constant battle between good and evil.

Ricardo Lopez, the victim of the brutal attack, lay in an ambulance gurney, his face a patchwork of bandages. Yet, despite the physical trauma, a flicker of defiance burned within him. Miraculously, he had survived the ordeal, and his testimony could be the key to unraveling the mystery surrounding the recent string of similar attacks. The victim described his attacker as a white male, slightly above average height, and slightly built. A distinct odor of wine or alcohol clung to the man's breath as he uttered that chilling phrase, "I will save you from Gehenna," during the assault.

This peculiar detail, along with the brutality of the attack, piqued the interest of Detective Zoe Baptiste. Zoe, a Creole woman with a deep-rooted connection to her Voodoo heritage, arrived at the crime scene with her partner, Detective Pete Foret. As she examined the gruesome report, a chill ran down her spine. The assault bore the hallmarks of a calculated, methodical act, eerily similar to the two previous attacks that had occurred over the last two weeks. A sense of dread washed over her as she realized they were dealing with a dangerous, possibly deranged individual. Zoe's intuition, honed by years of experience and a deep understanding of the supernatural, told her that there was more to this case than meets the eye. She sensed an evil entity lurking beneath the surface, a malevolent force driving the attacker to commit such heinous acts. As she delved deeper into the case notes, she knew she was treading on dangerous ground, a place where the lines between the natural and the supernatural routinely became blurred.

Intrigued by the word "Gehenna," Baptiste quickly jots it down in her small pocket notebook, determined to research it further when she returns to the office. The term resonates with her, sparking a sense of familiarity that she can't quite place. The first two victims had alluded to the attacker's phrase of "immense responsibilities" during their interviews, but this new term adds another layer to the puzzle. Her mind races as she considers the implications of this new connection.

With the investigation now spanning three victims, each having been assaulted but remarkably not killed, she senses that the attacker is motivated by something deeper, something tied to the dark forces that reverberate beneath the cracked streets of New Orleans. This city, rich in history and mystique, harbors secrets that Baptiste feels may be relevant to her case. In her quest for clarity, she decides to consult with her mother, a respected Voodoo Queen with a profound understanding of the supernatural and its influence on human behavior. Baptiste believes that her mother's wisdom could provide valuable insights into the nature of this anonymous attacker and potentially reveal his sinister motivations.

As she contemplates the possibility of involving her mother in the investigation, she feels a sense of urgency. Each assault leaves its stain on the community, and she is determined to prevent another incident. The knowledge that her mother possesses could

## CHAPTER 1: THE PHANTOM OF ORLEANS

illuminate the shadows cast by this enigmatic figure. She knows that in a city where the lines between the mundane and the mystical often blur, her mother's guidance and experience might be the key to unraveling this perplexing mystery. With a deep breath, she resolves to reach out to her mother as soon as possible, hoping for answers that could aid the New Orleans Police Department in their urgent pursuit of justice.

Later that evening, Baptiste finds herself sitting at her kitchen table, the faint glow of a single lamp casting warm light over her notebook filled with scribbled notes and theories. The word "Gehenna" looms large in her mind, along with the haunting stories of the victims. She takes a moment to breathe, allowing the weight of the case to settle. It's not just about the crimes; it's about the new fear that has gripped the community. She can't shake the feeling that the attacker is using the city's vibrant culture as a cover for something far more disturbing.

After gathering her thoughts, Baptiste picks up her phone and dials her mother's number. It rings a few times before her mother's voice, warm and wise, fills the air.

"Hello Mama, hope you're doing well. She continues, "Are you familiar with the recent string of assaults that have plagued the city? You know the ones that they have no suspects for yet?"

"I did jus' hear 'bout 'dat latest victim 'dat lost his eye." She continues, "Is 'dat your case, baby girl?"

"Yes, it is Mama. Pete and I are handling it right now, but we're stumped. Very little evidence and no real witnesses." She continues, "I wanted to pass something by you to see what you thought."

"Go 'head, Detective Baptiste," she playfully adds.

Zoe continues detailing the assaults along with the new mention of "Gehenna." Her mother listens intently, occasionally mur-

muring affirmations.

"Gehenna," she says, "Is a term steeped in darkness, and associated wit' judgment and da' afta-life. It could signify 'dat 'dis attacka' views his actions as a form of twisted retribution."

Intrigued, Zoe leans closer to the phone. "Do you think it's possible that he believes he's carrying out some kind of punishment?"

Her mother pauses, contemplating the question. "In 'da realm of spirits an' da unseen, 'dose who feel burdened by guilt or responsibility may act out in ways 'dat reflect 'deir inna' turmoil. You must consida' the spiritual energy of da' city—there are forces at play 'dat you may not fully unda-stand."

As they continue to converse, Zoe feels a sense of empowerment. Her mother's insights illuminate connections she hadn't considered before. Together, they devise a plan: Baptiste will revisit the crime scenes and gather more information while her mother prepares to perform a cleansing ritual to help clear any lingering negative energy. With a renewed sense of purpose, Baptiste hangs up the phone, ready to dive deeper into the case. She knows that with her mother's support, they might just uncover the truth behind the dark veil of the city—and, hopefully, bring peace to its restless souls. The investigation is far from over, but now Baptiste feels she has a guide through the shadows, and that makes all the difference.

Back at the office the following morning, Baptiste's mind buzzes with possibilities as she sits at her cluttered desk. With a determined look, she opens her laptop and begins to research the word "Gehenna," further. The results appear quickly, and she learns that it is a biblical term often used to describe a place of punishment or another classification for Hell itself. The connection strikes her with clarity; she remembers hearing the term during a mass she attended years ago. At that moment, it all began to click, the unsettling feeling she had about the attacks, the attacker's cryptic comments, and the underlying dark current that seemed to weave through the city's vibrant fabric.

Feeling another rush of urgency, Baptiste decides to reach out to a contact she has at the Archdiocese of New Orleans. She knows that the church often deals with matters that transcend the ordinary, particularly when it comes to issues of morality, spirituality, and the supernatural. After a few rings, her contact answers, and she quickly explains the situation, sharing her findings about the three assaults and the chilling reference to Gehenna. The tone of her voice conveys the gravity of her concerns, and she can sense her contact's growing interest.

They agreed to meet for a discussion. Baptiste prepares a concise presentation of her notes, organizing the details of the attacks and highlighting the connection to the term she had discovered. As she reviews her points, she wonders how the church might be able to assist. Could they provide insight into the spiritual ramifications of the attacks? Might there be clergy who specializes in such cases, possibly even exorcists? The questions swirled in her mind, each more pressing than the last.

Later, when they finally meet at the archdiocese's office, Baptiste is greeted warmly but with a sense of professionalism. The officials listen intently as she lays out her findings. After a thorough discussion, they agree that the situation is indeed unusual and merits attention. The local church representatives express their willingness to offer guidance and support in navigating the spiritual dimensions of the case. They assure her that they can provide resources, including consultations with knowledgeable clergy who can help understand the broader implications of what she's facing.

Feeling a mix of relief and gratitude, Baptiste leaves the meeting with a renewed sense of purpose. The church's involvement could offer new perspectives on the case, potentially revealing motivation behind the attacks that she hadn't considered. She knows that the path ahead will not be easy, but with the backing of both her mother's wisdom and the church's resources, she feels equipped to confront whatever darkness lies ahead. She knows that each step she takes brings her closer to uncovering the truth, and she is determined to protect her community from further harm.

The archbishop's decision to assist the department speaks volumes about the seriousness of the case at hand. Recognizing the intricate web of supernatural and psychological elements intertwined in the assaults, he designates Father Daryl Landry from St. Patrick's Church as Baptiste's Catholic advisor on the case. Father Landry is known for his deep faith and unwavering conviction, qualities that make him a trusted figure in the community. His spiritual guidance, coupled with a keen intellect, positions him as an invaluable resource in unraveling the enigma surrounding the phantom attacker.

As Baptiste prepares to reach out to Father Landry, she feels a mix of anticipation and hope. She understands that navigating the complexities of this case will require insights from multiple perspectives, and Landry's expertise in matters of faith could provide critical clues. After securing permission for the collaboration, she dials his number, her heart racing slightly as the phone rings. When Father Landry picks up, they exchange pleasantries, and Baptiste can't help but feel comforted by his warm demeanor.

Once the small talk subsides, Baptiste takes a deep breath and poses her question.

## CHAPTER 1: THE PHANTOM OF ORLEANS

"Father, are you familiar with the word 'Gehenna'?"

Without hesitation, he responds affirmatively, explaining that the term is well-known within Catholic teachings and is referenced several times in the New Testament, particularly in the Gospel of Mark. His voice is steady as he begins to share a brief history of the term, illuminating its significance as a representation of Hell. A place of punishment for the wicked.

As he elaborates, Baptiste listens intently, absorbing his insights. Father Landry explains that the term's roots lie in a valley near Jerusalem, historically associated with idolatry and the sacrifice of children, which eventually became synonymous with eternal damnation. He speculates that the individual behind the attacks might possess a deep understanding of both history and Catholic doctrine, suggesting a possible motive that ties into a warped sense of retribution or judgment.

She nods in agreement with Landry's analysis but feels a lingering uncertainty. While she values his perspective, she recognizes the importance of gathering additional viewpoints.

"Of course, I agree with you, Father," she replies thoughtfully. "But I'd still like to consult with my mother. With her Voodoo background, she has a unique understanding of the spiritual landscape here in New Orleans. The more angles we can explore, the better."

Father Landry respects her desire to seek another opinion, understanding that the complexities of the case might require insights that blend both spiritual and cultural perspectives. He reassures her that collaboration is crucial in investigations like this, where the line between physical and metaphysical are often convoluted. They discuss their next steps, and Baptiste relays an even more renewed sense of fortitude to her partner, Foret. This new team, comprised of the additions of Father Landry and her mother, should help to piece together the threads of this chilling mystery and ultimately protect the city from further harm.

The following day, Baptiste drives through the familiar streets of her city, a blend of excitement and trepidation swelling within her. As she approaches her mother's home, the vibrant colors and rich textures of the neighborhood wash over her, grounding her in the cultural tapestry that is so integral to her identity. She arrives at her old home and knocks on the front door. When no one answers, she walks around the side alley to enter the backyard, finally finding her mother relaxing to some local creole music. She steps inside the gate and the women enjoy a long, overdue embrace. The warmth of her mother's presence immediately put her at ease. Yemaya Baptiste, a wisewoman revered for her knowledge of the supernatural, steps back and greets her only daughter with a soft smile.

Once settled at the kitchen table, Zoe carefully shares some more key details about the case, mindful of the top-secret nature of the fledgling investigation. She emphasizes the importance of discretion, yet she knows her mother's insight could prove invaluable. Yemaya listens intently, her expression shifting as Zoe recounts the assaults and the chilling mention of Gehenna. Zoe notices the flicker of recognition in her mother's eyes; she now understands that this is no ordinary case.

Yemaya takes a moment to reflect on the information.

"Zo," she says thoughtfully, using Baptiste's nickname, "'Dis figure is likely not connected to the Voodoo arts as you might think. Voodoo practitioners typically have a different relationship with 'da spirits, one 'dat is rooted in respect and community. This person, whoever 'dey may be, seems to operate from a darker place." Her words resonate deeply with Baptiste, highlighting the com-

## CHAPTER 1: THE PHANTOM OF ORLEANS

plexity of the situation. She continues, "If 'da police could ever retrieve some sort of a personal item belonging to the attacka', I could discern whether 'dey have any ties to Voodoo or not. Objects carry energy, and I could read 'dat energy to understand their intentions and background."

Zoe nods, feeling a mix of hope and slight frustration. The notion of retrieving such an item feels daunting, yet she understands how crucial it could be to cracking the strange case.

Yemaya's insights align with what Father Landry had suggested.

"It's likely 'dat this attacka' is some sort of rogue Catholic," she agrees. "Someone who twists 'deir beliefs into something harmful. It's a dangerous blend of ideology and malice."

Zoe can't help but think of the shadows that seem to linger around the city, and how the vibrant culture often hides darker currents beneath the surface. Feeling a surge of gratitude for her mother's perspective, Baptiste leans in closer.

"Thank you, Mama. Your insights always help me see things more clearly."

They exchange a few more pleasantries, reminiscing about some family members that bring a smile to their faces amidst the weight of the conversation. As they finish their discussion, Zoe glances at the clock, realizing it's time to rejoin her partner, Pete Foret, who has been waiting outside. She steps out, finding him on the phone, his brow furrowed in concentration. He hangs up as she approaches, and she can sense his curiosity about her meeting with her mother. She takes a deep breath, ready to share the valuable insight she has gained, knowing that every piece of information could be vital in their quest to stop this anonymous attacker. Together, they prepare to delve deeper into the mystery that continues to shroud the Crescent City. As they walk to the car, Baptiste can see the sunlight filtering through the trees, casting dappled shade on the ground. The familiar sounds of the neighborhood—laughter, distant music, and the occasional chatter of vendors remind her of the city's radiant life. Yet beneath this lively facade lies an undercurrent of fear that she is determined to address. She approaches Pete, who is now pocketing his phone, his expression shifting to one of concern as he notices the seriousness in her eyes.

"So, what did your mom say?" he asks, his voice laced with curiosity.

Baptiste takes a moment to gather her thoughts, aware that the insights she's about to share could shift their investigation's trajectory.

"Quite a bit, actually," she begins, her tone earnest. "She doesn't believe the attacker is tied to Voodoo at all. Instead, she thinks this person operates from a dark, twisted understanding of Catholicism, like a rogue element of sort, who has taken universal beliefs and warped them into something sinister."

Pete raises an eyebrow, intrigued. "That aligns with what Father Landry mentioned. He felt the attacker might be using religious justification for their actions. It's unsettling."

Baptiste nods, feeling the weight of their findings settle heavily between them.

"I also talked to her about the importance of personal items," she continues. "She believes that if we could find something belonging to the attacker—like a piece of clothing or an item that they discarded, we could glean a lot about their motivations and possibly even their ties to the supernatural."

Pete ponders this for a moment, then scratches his chin. "That makes sense. If we can connect the dots between their actions and their beliefs, we might uncover more about their identity." He shifts his gaze toward the busy street, contemplating their next steps. "But how do we even start looking for a personal item without an identity? The attacks seem to have been random, and we don't have a clear suspect yet."

Baptiste sighs, feeling the challenge ahead. "We could start by revisiting the crime scenes. There might be overlooked details or evidence that could lead us to something personal left behind. Plus, we can engage the community more; someone may have seen something or know something. They just may be too scared to come forth right now."

Pete agrees, his expression is resolute. "Let's do it. The more eyes we have on this, the better chance we will have of finding something useful." He glances at his watch and adds, "We should move quickly. The longer we wait, the more likely it is that the trail will go cold."

Walking towards their car, Baptiste feels a sense of urgency driving her forward. She reflects on the conversations with her mother and Father Landry, feeling more equipped with the knowledge and perspectives they have shared. She always takes good notes, and she never forgets anything pertinent to her cases, and she's not going to change now. Baptiste and Pete will uncover the truth behind this madman.

Once inside the car, Baptiste maps out a plan.

"Let's hit the first two crime scenes and talk to the witnesses again. We can also look for any overlooked surveillance footage nearby, anything that might give us a clue about who was around during the attacks."

"Sounds good to me," Pete replies, while starting the engine.

As they drive through the lively streets of New Orleans, Baptiste glances out the window, taking in the sights and sounds once again. She knows that the city holds many secrets, and she is determined to uncover them, not just for the sake of the case, but for the safety of the community she loves. With each passing block, her resolve strengthens. She is ready to face the darkness, armed with the insights of those who understand both the spiritual and earthly realms. Together, she feels they are prepared to navigate whatever challenges lie ahead, determined to protect the innocent and bring justice to those affected by the recent assaults.

As the investigation deepens, the city's occupants seem to hold their breath, collectively waiting for the day when this serial attacker's reign of terror will come to an end. The atmosphere is charged with a sense of unease, each day passing like a weight hanging over the community. People move cautiously through the streets, exchanging worried glances and hushed whispers. The bright energy that usually fills the air has shifted, replaced by a substantial tension as citizens grapple with the uncertainty of their safety.

The news of the most recent brutal attack spreads like wildfire, igniting a wave of panic throughout the neighborhoods. Social media buzzes with alerts and warnings, amplifying the fear that has begun to seep into everyday life. Community forums fill with discussions about safety precautions, and local businesses post notices urging patrons to remain vigilant. Families huddle together in their homes, locking doors and drawing curtains as if that could somehow shield them from the darkness that has descended upon their city. Fear grips the hearts of the residents, as questions swirl through the community. Who is the next victim? Where will this phantom strike next? The sheer unpredictability of the attacks

## CHAPTER 1: THE PHANTOM OF ORLEANS

only intensifies the anxiety, creating an atmosphere where everyone feels like a potential target. Parents keep a tighter grip on their children's hands, and friends refuse to part ways after dark. The once radiant nightlife of New Orleans dims as many choose to stay indoors, hoping to avoid becoming a headline in the local news.

Amid this turmoil, pressure mounts on the police department. Each day that passes without an arrest feels like a failure, a reminder of this phantom attacker lurking seemingly just out of reach. The officers work tirelessly, sifting through evidence and following leads that often seem to lead nowhere. They are met with a wall of silence from the community, as fear has silenced many who might have spoken up. Neighbors who once knew each other now exchange wary glances, hesitant to engage in conversation about the ongoing terror.

Despite the mounting pressure, the police remain resolute. They hold community meetings to encourage residents to share any information, no matter how small. Yet, the responses are sparse, the fear too great to overcome the instinct for self-preservation. Baptiste and Foret feel the weight of the community's anxiety on their shoulders. They know that the clock is ticking and that each moment without resolution increases the risk of another attack.

As Baptiste reflects on the growing gravity of the situation, she feels and knows the investigation has become more than just another tough case, it's also about restoring safety and peace to a city that has been shaken to its core. She understands that they must find a way to break through silence and fear, to connect with the community and encourage them to share their stories. It's a daunting task, but she knows that they cannot solve this mystery alone. Together, they strategize on how to reach out to the public, considering community events and local gatherings where people might feel more comfortable discussing their fears. They plan to partner with group leaders who can help bridge the gap between the police and the residents, fostering an environment where information can flow more freely. With each passing hour, the stakes become higher. As the sun sets over the city, casting long shadows through the streets, Baptiste readies herself for the tasks ahead. She knows that the path will be fraught with barriers, but she is committed to facing the evil head-on and winning.

Baptiste, Foret, and Father Landry work tirelessly, dedicating themselves to solving this case that has left the city in turmoil. Each day, they gather in the dimly lit precinct, fueled by a mix of determination and desperation. Their collaboration has become a crucial lifeline in the investigation, as they pool their skills and insights to chase down every lead. The trio interviews the few witnesses who are willing to share their experiences, hoping to extract even the slightest detail that could illuminate the assaulter's identity. Each interview feels like a race against time, the weight of the city's anxiety pressing down on them.

Despite their efforts, this phantom seems to have vanished into thin air, leaving behind no trace of his identity. Baptiste feels a growing frustration as leads fizzle out, and potential suspects turn out to be useless. As the days go by, the air of tension in the precinct clots. The detectives spend countless hours poring over numerous photos of the crime scenes and the victim's wounds, analyzing every detail with relentless scrutiny. They meticulously compile reports, cross-referencing evidence in hopes of identifying a pattern or connection that might have eluded them so far.

With each passing day, the city grows increasingly anxious. News coverage remains relentless, and the public's fear is uncontrollable. The once-bustling streets now seem even quieter,

## CHAPTER 1: THE PHANTOM OF ORLEANS

with residents hesitant to venture out after dark. Baptiste feels the weight of this fear, a constant reminder of the stakes involved in their investigation. She knows that without resolution, the likelihood of more attacks is imminent, and that thought keeps her up at night.

This phantom of sorts has become a specter haunting the streets of New Orleans, a ghost that slips through their fingers no matter how hard they try to grasp it. He symbolizes the crime that lurks throughout the city blocks, but his attacks are more unexplainable than the usual crimes that plague this historic city. The juxtaposition of the joy of her doing the job she loves and the terror of this soon-to-be landmark of a case, weighs heavily on Baptiste's heart, a constant reminder that not everything is as it seems.

In their quest for answers, the detectives begin to look beyond the obvious. They dive into the histories of the victims, searching for common threads that might hint at a motive. They explore the neighborhoods where the assaults occurred, speaking with locals in hopes of uncovering something, anything that could lead them to their ghost. Each interaction is an opportunity, and Baptiste remains determined to connect with the community, encouraging them to share their thoughts and concerns.

They turn even more of their attention to the spiritual elements of the case. Father Landry's insights resonate deeply with Baptiste. Together, they greatly feel that this phantom's actions are probably being influenced by beliefs rooted in a distorted understanding of his faith. They discuss the implications of Gehenna and how it may tie into the attacker's psyche. Landry suggests that delving into the religious aspects of the case could yield even more perspectives and lead them down unforeseen paths.

But even with these fresh angles, the elusive attacker remains just that—elusive. Each time they think they have a decent lead, it just slips away, leaving them more frustrated than before. Baptiste feels the pressure mounting not only from her superiors, but also from the neighbors she knows in the community, looking to them for answers. The weight of their responsibility grows heavier, but so does their resolution. They refuse to let this phantom person remain an unchecked threat, and they are determined not to let fear overshadow their purpose. Baptiste rallies her team, reminding them of the lives they are fighting for. She reminds them that they have the power to make the difference, and with every small step, they inch closer to the truth. They know this case can be taxing and demoralizing, but she reminds the whole department that persistence is key. And in a city as resilient as New Orleans, they will ultimately find a way to confront the demon lurking in the shadows.

The presumed attacker sits in the dim light of his small, cluttered apartment, transfixed by the flickering images on the television screen. The local news coverage details his latest heinous assault, and a twisted grin spreads across his face, reflecting a disturbing sense of satisfaction. Each word of the report fills him with pride as the anchors refer to him with a mix of fear and fascination. One channel dubs him the "Phantom of Orleans," while another network labels him the "Crescent City Prowler." Both names carry a weight of infamy, and he savors the notoriety, relishing the chaos he has unleashed upon the unsuspecting city. Though excited, he must remember that he is not just feeding his ego. This duty is to appease the Lord, his Father, and to rescue his fellow fallen sheep of the flock.

The news anchors issue stern warnings to the public, urging them to remain vigilant and aware of their surroundings. They

## CHAPTER 1: THE PHANTOM OF ORLEANS

recount the details of his three successful attacks, each executed with chilling efficiency and precision, leaving no trace behind. He watches as they replay grainy footage from security cameras, his heart racing with adrenaline at the thought of how close he came to being caught. The description of his methods—quick, calculated, and utterly anonymous. This makes him feel invincible, as if he has transcended the ordinary boundaries of morality and consequence. In his mind, he is not just a criminal; he is an artist of fear, crafting a narrative that keeps the city on edge.

As the frantic updates draw to a close, the mood shifts in the room. The thrill of his accomplishments begins to give way to something deeper, a stirring within him that cannot be ignored. He slides from the sofa, his movements deliberate and measured, as he drops to his knees on the worn carpet. The shadows of the room seem to close in around him, but instead of feeling confined, he finds a strange comfort in the darkness. He tilts his head upward, gazing into the dimness above, as if searching for some divine acknowledgment of his actions. With a fervent intensity, he begins to recite the "Our Father" prayer aloud, his voice low but steady, reverberating through the silent apartment. The words roll off his tongue, a ritual he has adopted as part of his twisted justification for the terror he has inflicted. As he prays, he imagines himself standing in a sacred space, enveloped by an otherworldly presence that endorses his endeavors. He envisions his actions as a form of divine retribution, a cleansing of sorts, though the irony of his prayer is lost on him. Each phrase of the prayer resonates within him, intertwining with his dark motivations. He believes he is doing God's work, an instrument of fate punishing those he deems unworthy. His heart races with excitement as he imagines the fear he has instilled in the city, the power he holds over its inhabitants.

With every word, he feels emboldened, convinced that his mission is righteous.

As he finishes the Lord's prayer, a sense of calm washes over him, mingling with the thrill of his violent deeds. The shadows in the room seem to stretch and retreat, momentarily illuminating his face as if casting him in a spotlight. He rises slowly, the flickering television casting an eerie glow, and for a moment, he allows himself to bask in the satisfaction of his dual existence—a man of prayer and a harbinger of fear. The dichotomy fuels his resolve, and he prepares for whatever comes next, confident that the Phantom of Orleans is far from done.

# CHAPTER 2: HIS REIGN AND REPUTATION GROWS

New Orleans was gripped by an unrelenting fear. The specter of the Phantom, a moniker bestowed upon the elusive assailant by the local news and media, cast a long shadow over the city. This enigmatic figure had emerged from the darkness, striking with chilling regularity, leaving a trail of terror and despair in his wake. The victims, both men and women from all walks of life, were found mutilated and maimed, their bodies bearing the grotesque hallmarks of a brutal and calculated attack. The police department, despite their tireless efforts, were baffled by the Phantom's methods. Their investigations led them down countless dead ends, leaving them with more questions than answers. The only discernible pattern among the growing number of victims was their shared involvement in questionable activities prior to the attacks. It seemed as though this Phantom was a type of vigilante, a self-appointed judge and jury, punishing those he deemed deserving of retribution. Yet, a peculiar twist to this macabre tale was that none of the victims had ever been killed. While this may have offered a slight glimmer of hope, it was a cold comfort for those who were left to endure the physical and psychological scars inflicted upon them. Some might even argue that a swift death would have been a more merciful fate than the horrific injuries and disabilities that they were now forced to live with.

Detectives Baptiste and Foret are working tirelessly on the case as usual. But the Phantom seems to have left no real vestige. As they are reviewing the growing case files, Baptiste states what they know up to this point aloud to Pete yet again.

"Okay, most of the victims have been attacked in secluded areas, far from the prying eyes of witnesses. So, he is probably a local who knows the city well. A person who is very familiar with all of the city cameras and which angles afford him the best chances of remaining anonymous. He knows the city like the back of his hand."

Foret replies, "It's most likely, but we've checked all the local records, and no one fits the description. He doesn't have a record either. All we know is that he doesn't like sinners, which basically means he doesn't like anyone, and that he has an unlimited number of targets, especially in this town."

She responds, "We need to think outside of the box. Are there any other connections between the victims that we aren't seeing? Do they share a secret, or perhaps they are all involved together in something illegal?"

"It's a long shot," he admits. "But I really don't think so. We've cross-referenced their lives over a hundred times. No hidden pasts, no shared secrets. It's as if they were just random targets, chosen by chance."

Baptiste is more alarmed, "Or perhaps not by chance. Maybe

there's another sick pattern we're missing. Something subtle, something only the Phantom sees."

"Like what," he answers. "A specific trait, a shared belief? Something that marks them as sinners in his eyes?"

Baptiste leans forward, "It could be anything. A certain type of clothing, a particular accessory. Maybe even a very specific behavior or mannerism."

Foret confused, "We've checked their social media, their online activity. Nothing really stands out. It's like he's hunting ghosts."

Baptiste pushes back, "Or perhaps he's creating them. Maybe he's driving people to despair, making them into the sinners he wants to punish. And if so, why is he telling them that he's helping them? How in the hell is maiming someone actually helping them?"

Agreeing Foret jumps in, "A psychological tormentor. A master manipulator. That would explain the lack of physical evidence. No trace, quick with no tangible connection."

Baptiste again determined; "We need to talk to the survivors again. I know it's hard for some of them to relive this, but maybe they can shed some more light on this asshole's motives. Perhaps they've seen something minute, heard something that we've missed."

"It's worth a shot," he agrees. "But we have to be careful. That bastard is watching, always watching. One wrong move, and we could even become the next target."

"I'd like to see him try," she quickly retorts. "We'd have this case over a lot sooner, I'll tell you that," she adds defiantly.

Together, they continue their deep dive into the personal lives of the victims, determined to uncover any hidden connections that could lead them to their guy. They began a series of even more detailed interviews, speaking with friends, family, and co-workers, meticulously piecing together the last moments leading up to each victim's ordeal. Each conversation revealed a new layer, a glimpse into the victims' personalities and their relationships. Yet, despite their efforts, the information often felt disjointed, as if they were trying to assemble a jigsaw puzzle with missing pieces.

As they combed through the monotonous interviews, Baptiste felt a growing sense of frustration. They secretly prayed for any link between the cases to appear, but their prayers continue to go unanswered. The victims seemed ordinary, with no apparent ties to one another beyond their tragic fates. While some friends spoke of minor conflicts or disagreements, nothing substantial surfaced—no mutual acquaintances, no shared secrets. The deeper they probed, the more elusive this Phantom became. Unlike other cases where perpetrators left behind cryptic clues or taunted authorities with ominous messages, this assailant operated with chilling precision and anonymity. It was as if he had carefully planned each attack, erasing any trace of his existence, leaving the detectives with nothing but disgust and questions.

Baptiste couldn't shake the feeling that the Phantom was relishing his victories. He had successfully evaded capture, and the dread he instilled in the community was growing. It was a haunting realization; everyone seemed to know it, even the detectives themselves. As they continued their reviews, she imagined the Phantom watching from the dark, reveling in his success, pleased with the chaos he had sown. Each day that passed without an arrest felt like a silent acknowledgment of his triumph.

With each discussion, Baptiste and Foret pushed themselves harder, their determination unwavering despite the mounting pressure. They began brainstorming ideas that extended beyond the obvious, questioning everything they thought they knew about the victims repeatedly. Discussing the possibility of a hidden agenda, a secret life that none of their loved ones had been aware of. They couldn't afford to overlook anything. As frustration swirled in the air, Baptiste found a flicker of hope: perhaps the key to unraveling the mystery may lie right in front of them, just waiting to be uncovered. Only time would tell...but unfortunately, time was not a luxury they had.

Could there be a local, contrary religious group or cult known for their extreme views and secretive nature? This was one of the many questions that lingered in the back of Zoe's mind as she and Foret sifted through leads and analyzed every shred of information they could find. Such groups often operated off the grid, their members bound by secrecy and an unwavering allegiance to their beliefs, making them nearly invisible to the outside world. As the worn-down detectives delve deeper into the social fabric of the troubled community, they considered the possibility that the Phantom might be linked to a radical group whose ideology placed a twisted emphasis on morality, viewing his violent acts as a form of purification or absolution.

They had to keep digging, fueled by an unyielding purpose to bring this mysterious figure to justice, no matter how daunting the task seemed. With each passing day, he was slipping further from their grasp, his movements always unpredictable. The mounting pressure of the investigation weighed heavily on both detectives, but Baptiste refused to let despair set in. They began canvassing local neighborhoods, seeking out any whispers from fringe groups or unsanctioned gatherings that could provide a clue. Every encounter, every conversation felt charged with potential, yet often left them feeling more disheartened. This part of the community was tight-lipped, wary of outsiders, and Baptiste knew that breaking through this veil of secrecy would be no easy feat. With the clock ticking and each day drawing them closer to another potential attack, the stakes felt impossibly high. They knew that if they didn't score soon, the Phantom would continue to wreak havoc, emboldened by his seeming invincibility. Determined to uncover the truth, the detectives dug deeper into local lore, historical records, and online forums, hoping to find even a hint that might lead them closer to understanding the mind of this lunatic and the dark motivations driving his atrocious actions.

Zoe, always intrigued by investigating the local lore of the city, feels that she needs to commune again with her mother, Yemaya, the Voodoo-strong wisewoman for additional advice, as more victims are maimed throughout the city. The department is perplexed because no one is ever killed or robbed. The victims all have some body part severely injured or removed, and they all have mentioned hearing either the word "Gehanna", or his eerie catch phrase: "I've been entrusted with immense responsibility." There doesn't seem to be any link between race or gender with the attacks either, they have happened to people of all colors and genders. The only one glaring similarity is that most of the time these victims are usually involved in risqué' extracurricular activities leading up to the assault. It's times like this that Zoe is grateful for her mother and Father Landry's expertise, they are so very important to aiding this tiresome investigation.

The news media and the public continue to be absorbed by the unknown, their anxious whispers echoing through the streets. Everyone's daily routines are interrupted by the ominous presence of the Phantom. And in her mother's home, Zoe could feel the tension radiating from Yemaya, who sat with a furrowed brow,

## CHAPTER 2: HIS REIGN AND REPUTATION GROWS

watching the latest news updates flash across the tv screen.

Her mom breaking the silence, "Zo, I still really don't think this is Voodoo related," her voice steady but firm. "If it were, the victims wouldn't just be injured. 'Dere would likely be death, kidnapping and panic resulting from some supernatural spells or dark magic. 'Dis doesn't have 'da signs of anything mystical; it's methodical and calculated."

Zoe crossed her arms, frustration creeping into her tone. "But Mom, how can you be so sure? Just because it doesn't fit the 'normal' modus operandi, it doesn't mean it isn't a related dark ritual. He's using fear as a weapon as well. You always say that fear can be just as powerful as any spell."

Her mother sighed, clearly trying to remain patient.

"I understand your point baby, but we must be practical. You know as well as I do 'dat the true nature of 'dese attacks seems more rooted in something human, something that doesn't rely on 'da magic or of 'da supernatural." Closing her eyes and slowly exhaling, she continues, "It feels like a personal vendetta of some sort, rather 'dan a ritualistic sacrifice or slaughta'."

Zoe, intrigued again, asks, "So, what are you saying? He's just a regular person who's snapped. That he's not some sort of dark sorcerer?"

"Basically," her mom replied, her eyes narrowing slightly as she thought about the case. She continues, "What we need to focus on is the psychology behind his actions. Remember, if you ever can get some-'ding personal of the attacka'—like a token or a clue of sort—we might be able to understand his motives better 'trough vibrations in 'da universe. With faith and proper incantations, we may be able to feel where his location is, or we might even gain a hint of who he may be."

Zoe considered this, her mind racing again with possibilities. "So, we really need to stay thorough, we need him to leave us a physical clue or something personal, something with his energy around it."

"Precisely," her mom encouraged. "'Dink about it. 'Dat item combined wit' a pattern or connection wit' 'dese victims 'dat you may have missed at 'dis time, could lead us straight to him. He may have a histry' wit' 'dem, since 'dey are usually involved in some-'ting 'dat has attracted his attention."

"But how do we get to that point?" Zoe asked, a mix of anxiety and determination in her voice. "We've already checked countless times on whether there are any connections between him and the victims, and we've found nothing. Plus, we can't just sit back and wait for him to leave us a tangible item or for the next terrible news report. We need to do something now."

Her mother nodded, her expression softening. "I know it feels overwhelming my dear, but we must approach 'dis carefully. Gathering information requires subtlety, not just panic-driven actions. If we can keep our eyes open and stay calm, we might just find 'da missin' piece of 'dis puzzle. Patience baby."

Zoe took a deep breath, feeling a surge of calm resolve. "Okay, we'll continue looking even deeper into the backgrounds of the victims again. Maybe there's some small thing we've missed in their lives that can shed light on this. If we can find that small connection, we'll be one step closer to bagging his ass."

Yemaya smiled, the tension in the room easing slightly. "'Dat's 'da spirit! United, we can piece together 'da clues, no matta' how small. Keep an eye out for any personal items, but be careful and always trust your instincts. 'Dey have always served you well, my sweet child."

## CHAPTER 2: HIS REIGN AND REPUTATION GROWS

With a revived sense of purpose, Zoe felt ready to tackle the investigation head-on again, determined to reclaim a sense of safety for herself and her city.

In the background, the local news blared from the television, casting a flickering light across the room. The top two stories dominated the broadcast, both intricately tied to the growing shadow of the newly labeled Phantom. The first segment featured the mayor, his face drawn and serious, as he spoke with a local action reporter about the economic fallout from the Phantom's reign of terror.

"We're seeing a significant decline in tourism," he stated, his voice heavy with concern. "With fewer people willing to venture out, businesses are suffering. Local shops, restaurants, and attractions are all feeling the impact. We need to find a way to restore confidence in our community."

As the mayor continued to outline the grim statistics, Zoe felt a sense of unease wash over her. The Phantom wasn't just a danger to individuals; he was now a threat to the very livelihood of the city. The news report painted a stark picture: empty streets, shuttered storefronts, and an atmosphere thick with fear. It was a chilling reminder that the effects of the Phantom's actions reached far beyond the immediate violence, plunging the city into an economic downturn that no one could afford to ignore.

The second story that flashed across the screen shifted the mood dramatically. It covered the conclusion of the high-profile bribery trial of subjugated Officer Blain Casey, a known corrupt cop. The scene outside the historic Broad St. courthouse was chaotic, with a throng of reporters clamoring for attention, cameras flashing as they captured every moment. Zoe's interest peaked as she watched her fellow officer, Casey, emerge down the courthouse stairs, flanked by her legal team, a self-satisfied smile plastered on her face. It was hard to believe that this woman, who had been caught red-handed in her corrupt dealings, was walking free once again.

The news anchor detailed how Casey had skillfully navigated her way out of almost certain conviction by habitually lying on the stand.

"Her tactics almost certainly included threatening certain jurors and reportedly bribing others along with crucial city officials," the anchor explained, the incredulity evident in her tone.

Zoe couldn't shake the feelings of outrage and disgust as she watched the scene unfold. It was as if justice had been twisted and warped, and those who were supposed to uphold the law were instead undermining it. It felt similar to what the Phantom was committing, just a different version of misconduct. Even though she had known Casey for years, she couldn't help feeling disappointed after hearing the outcome. *If anyone needed to be punished, it was definitely Casey.*

As the video continued, Casey stepped into the waiting car, a slimy lawyer by her side, smiling with smugness radiating from her. The cameras captured her waving to the crowd, a display of triumph that only fueled Zoe's displeasure. *How could someone so blatantly corrupt escape accountability while the city suffered under the grip of the Phantom?* The juxtaposition of the two stories - the economic despair caused by the Phantom and the brazen freedom of a crooked officer - left Zoe feeling helpless yet determined. She knew that this was a pivotal moment for her city, and she was resolute in her desire to uncover the truth behind both the Phantom and the corruption that seemed to plague their system.

The following day, the radios and televisions across the city

## CHAPTER 2: HIS REIGN AND REPUTATION GROWS

crackled to life with breaking news that sent shockwaves through the community. Reports flooded in that Officer Blain Casey had been rushed to the hospital after a brutal attack. The details were grim: she had apparently lost one of her ears at the hands of the mysterious Phantom. As the story unfolded, the city held its breath. Many locals were stunned by the violence, their initial shock giving way to a mix of disbelief and intrigue. However, to the surprise of some, there were others who couldn't suppress their sense of slight satisfaction at the news.

In cafes, bars, and homes, conversations erupted. *"Finally, someone is making her pay for what she did!"* one man declared, his voice tinged with vindication. Others nodded in agreement, recalling the myriad ways Casey had manipulated the law and the people she was sworn to protect. For many, the Phantom's actions were being framed as a form of tough justice, a vigilante taking matters into his own hands where the system had failed. It was a disturbing twist in the narrative; rather than fearing the Phantom, some citizens were starting to see him as a necessary evil, a tainted protector in a wounded city that felt increasingly corrupt and unsafe-even if partially caused by him.

This new perception of the Phantom posed a significant challenge for the detectives on the case. Baptiste and Foret had always approached their work with the belief that justice must be served through legal channels. But now, with the community seemingly divided in its response, they faced a complex web of moral ambiguity. If the locals began to rally around the Phantom, viewing him as a hero rather than a villain, it could hinder their investigation. Witnesses who might have been willing to share information could very well clam up, reluctant to aid in the capture of someone they viewed as an unlikely protector of the people.

As the news spread, Baptiste and Foret realized they needed to adapt their approach. They gathered at their precinct, grappling with the implications of the public's shifting sentiment. The detectives needed to remind the community that vigilante justice often came with dangerous consequences. What might feel like retribution to some could escalate into chaos, undermining the very fabric of law and order. The situation required a delicate balance; they had to investigate the Phantom while simultaneously addressing the community's newfound fascination with him. The detectives' phones buzzed with tips and rumors, but Baptiste felt a bit uneasy. With every passing hour, the line between right and wrong blurred further. The Phantom was no longer just a threat; for some, he had become a symbol of rebellion against a system that many felt had failed them. They needed to get to the bottom of this quickly—before the city devolved into a lawless arena where the lines between hero and villain became dangerously indistinct.

Baptiste sat at her desk, staring at the reports that piled up in front of her, each detailing the bizarre events surrounding Officer Blain Casey's attack. The entire department was abuzz with confusion and speculation. *Why had the Phantom chosen to remove her ear?* It was a brutal act that seemed to carry a specific message, yet the motives behind it remained elusive. Casey was undeniably a dirty cop, and Baptiste found it difficult to muster any pity for her. Many in the department had long felt that Casey had escaped justice time and time again, skirting the consequences of her corrupt actions with a mix of deceit, bribery, blackmail, and intimidation. But there were also some fellow officers that had her back no matter what. She was one of them, and it seemed that because her father was a retired officer, she was always going to get help from behind the scenes. There was a small divide that had taken shape

## CHAPTER 2: HIS REIGN AND REPUTATION GROWS

in the department, but it is even more prominent now. Yet, even with people choosing what side they were on, the main question lingered: why this particular form of retribution?

As the days went on, Baptiste couldn't shake the unsettling thought that the Phantom was, in a way, gaining traction as a vigilante. The public's response to Casey's injury had been mixed, with some segments of the community expressing a troubling admiration for the masked figure who had dealt out a punishment they felt was long overdue. This shift in perception was alarming; it suggested that the Phantom was not just operating outside the law but stepping into a role that many had unconsciously wished for—a dark savior capable of exacting justice in a system perceived as a corrupt joke. It raised difficult questions for Baptiste and her team: could the Phantom finish what the department had struggled to do for so long?

The idea that a vigilante could be seen as a solution to the city's corruption was both intoxicating and terrifying. It forced the detectives to confront their own beliefs about justice and morality. If the Phantom was indeed viewed as a hero by some, it could severely complicate their investigation. Witnesses who might otherwise have cooperated could remain silent, unwilling to assist in apprehending someone they believed was serving a greater purpose. The tension between law enforcement and the community was undeniable, and Baptiste knew that navigating this new landscape would require not just skill, but a deep understanding of the evolving dynamics at play. She feared that the consequences could spiral out of control if they didn't act decisively.

Father Landry arrived at the office, and Baptiste wasted no time in asking him the same burning question. "Why would he cut off Casey's ear, Father?"

Landry considered the question for a moment before responding. "It's probably his version of ear cropping."

Foret interjected, his brow furrowed in confusion. "You mean like what they do to dogs?"

"Well, kind of," Landry clarified. "You see, this ear cropping was a form of punishment from the 18th century. It was used for crimes such as counterfeiting money, perjury, or arson. As for Officer Casey, take your pick of what charge she was punished for. But my money's on her committing perjury."

Foret nodded, his eyes wide. "Either the Phantom is a serious history buff, or we have a very determined vigilante on the loose."

Landry nodded in agreement. "This is yet another example of the victims in these cases having committed some sort of crime against society and/or the Lord God."

After a few moments of silence, Baptiste brandished a clear evidence bag containing a black, double-edged dagger.

"Look what we got this time, Father," she said, her eyes sparkling with excitement.

Landry leaned in, his expression shifting. "Is that what I think it is?"

Baptiste smiled. "It sure is. You see, during the attack on our very own Officer Casey, she managed to wrestle and attain one of the Phantom's knives before he hastily left. Of course, there are no fingerprints, but at least now Pete and I can bring it to my mom."

"That's wonderful news," Landry replied, his voice filled with enthusiasm.

They now had the personal item of the Phantom that Yemaya needed to analyze.

Later that day, Baptiste carefully placed the evidence bag containing the knife on the table in front of her mother, Yemaya. The room was dimly lit, the air thick with the scent of herbs and the lingering smoke from incense. Yemaya sat cross-legged on the floor, surrounded by chicken blood and bleached bones, her eyes focused intently on the captured weapon.

"Are you ready for this, Mom?" Baptiste asked, her voice a mix of excitement and apprehension.

Yemaya nodded, her expression serious. "I am. But remember, the energies we're about to uncover might reveal truths you're not prepared for."

Zoe took a deep breath, watching as her mother began to chant a series of unrecognizable terms, her voice rhythmic and powerful. It had been quite a few years since she last sat in on one of her mother's seances. She remembered the smells and the intensity with what her mother orchestrated the dark sessions with. The light smoky clouds that formed around the table seemed to dance in response to Yemaya's incantations. After a few minutes, Yemaya's eyes fluttered closed, and Zoe could see the tension in her mother's face as she entered a deeper state of concentration.

Finally, Yemaya opened her eyes, a glimmer of clarity shining through. "I see something," she said, her voice steady yet tinged with urgency. "From 'da indications I just envisioned, I can all but guarantee 'dat my initial feelings were correct. This Phantom is not of my beloved Voodoo community."

Zoe's heart raced. "What do you mean? Are you sure?"

Yemaya continued her gaze distant. "I visualize a large stone cross, just like the ones found all over Catholic churches. 'Dere's an undeniable symbolism tied to it. 'Dis is no mere act of vengeance; 'dis man is driven by a twisted sense of righteousness."

"So, you're saying he's a religious fanatic?" Baptiste asked, her mind running with the implications.

"Yes," Yemaya affirmed, her voice firm. "Our famous vigilante is probably a Christian religious zealot. 'Dis isn't just personal for him; it's a crusade of sorts. And 'dat makes him even more dangerous."

Zoe relaxed and leaned back, absorbing the weight of her mother's words. "What do we do with this new information? How do we stop him if he believes he's on a holy mission?"

Yemaya sighed at the gravity of the situation evident in her expression. "We must tread carefully. Understanding his motivations is crucial, but we need to ensure 'dat we don't fall into his trap. Vigilantes believe 'dey are untouchable, and 'dat gives 'dem power. We must approach 'dis wit' caution, my sweet Zoe."

"I'll do whatever it takes," she replied, determination igniting within her. "Mama, we need to protect the city, and I won't let him continue his crusade unchecked."

As Zoe drove home from her mother's house, her mind swirled with a cacophony of thoughts, each one colliding with the next like the raindrops that streamed down her windshield. The rhythmic patter of the rain created a soothing backdrop, lulling her into a meditative state as she navigated the slick streets. She watched the world outside transform into a blur of colors, the headlights of passing cars refracting through the droplets, creating a kaleidoscope effect that mirrored her tumultuous emotions. The weight of her mother's revelations pressed heavily on her mind; the idea that the Phantom was not just a criminal, or a vigilante to some, he was also a fanatical religious zealot as well. What kind of man would justify violence in the name of his faith?

The rain became a metaphor for her worries, each drop representing a question she couldn't quite answer. She gripped the steering wheel tighter, her knuckles whitening as she considered the implications of her mother's words. The city felt different somehow, cloaked in a sense of foreboding, and as the wipers swished rhythmically, she couldn't shake the feeling that she was racing against time. She needed to connect the dots before the Phantom's next move—before more lives were affected, including her own.

# CHAPTER 3: DEVILISH DEACON?

The investigation had dragged on for weeks now, with little progress beyond a tangled web of clues that seemed to lead nowhere. Every lead ended in the usual dead end, each witness more frightened or less reliable than the last. The city had been on edge ever since the first assaults were tied to the Phantom, a vigilante figure who seemed to strike at those he considered to be morally corrupt. The victims were discovered in semi-public places, their maimed bodies on display, sending a message to a cruel audience: If you were a sinner in the eyes of the Phantom, you best be aware of your surroundings. Because he could strike anyone, anytime, and that even went for anybody in the city's underworld, corrupt politicians, as well as crooked businesspeople. It could be anybody, because everyone fits his unspoken criteria. But the complexity of the assaults made it unclear whether the Phantom was targeting specific individuals, or whether he was simply casting a wider net like a shadow sweeping over the city's

## CHAPTER 3: DEVILISH DEACON?

entire moral fabric, waiting to snare anyone who strayed too far from the light.

Detectives Baptiste and Foret were seasoned investigators who had seen their fair share of crime. They now find themselves navigating an increasingly bizarre case. The pattern was maddeningly inconsistent, with no clear connection between the victims except for their presumed moral failings. The Phantom wasn't just another murderer or criminal mastermind; this was someone with a clear, twisted sense of justice. There were no senseless crimes here; each attack felt deliberate, with intention woven into every gruesome detail. Each crime scene seemed like a grotesque, religious illustration. They were haunting, as though he was trying to create a real-life macabre performance that twisted scripture into a bloodstained mockery of redemption. With each new redemptive crime, the detectives believed they were chasing a person who saw himself as a soldier of the Lord, or an obedient religious visionary. They were dealing with someone who believed he was the acting hand of God Himself, meting out divine retribution. Unbeknownst to them, he wasn't just punishing his victims, the Phantom felt that he was vindicating them from Hell as well.

Baptiste, distraught but silent, was beginning to question how much longer they could maintain their composure under the strain of the endless case. Every day without a breakthrough felt like a small failure, a blow to their already fragile sense of control. The pressure from the media, the public outcry, and the unanswered questions were taking their toll. She could feel it gnawing at her, like an itch that she couldn't scratch, the weight of the case settling deeper into her bones. Foret, by contrast, had an even bigger edge to himself now, constantly pacing the office, muttering about the impossible nature of the case. His temper was shorter, his patience thinning, and she could see it in the way her partner's hands trembled as he rifled through evidence files.

"We're no closer to finding this bastard than we were the day it started," Foret had snapped that morning, his voice tinged with frustration. "We're playing catch-up, and it's a game we're going to lose if we don't start getting real answers, fast."

Now, through the department's relentless deep undercover work and some light intel provided by Father Landry, Zoe and Pete begin to home in on a local Catholic deacon known to push the envelope when speaking on subjects such as sinners being punished, revelation, and people accepting their due penance.

Deacon Carlos Mancini is known to press the boundaries of religious rhetoric, often speaking about sinners being chastised and the importance of repentance, sometimes severe. Many of his parishioners are turned off by his fiery and controversial sermons and his unorthodox, loud, aggressive and intimidating demeanor. Some children are even scared to attend mass when he presides over that day's service. Could this be the wolf in sheep's clothing that they've been searching for? His personality and his stature sure seem to fit the Phantom's profile. Even if he wasn't the famed attacker, he may at least know of him or the secret group that he may operate out of.

The detectives knew they had to dig deeper into Deacon Mancini's background. After weeks of sifting through church records and speaking with local parishioners, they decided to take a more direct approach.

They began attending a few of his weekly services. Mancini, with his large frame, booming voice and commanding presence, had a reputation as a charismatic figure in the community. His sermons were filled with fervor, his words often carrying the weight

## CHAPTER 3: DEVILISH DEACON?

of moral judgment that seemed to resonate with most of the congregation. Baptiste and Foret sat in the pews, blending in with the regular parishioners, observing the man from a distance. But despite their best efforts to observe him objectively, the feeling that something wasn't quite right continued to linger.

After several services, the detectives manage to arrange a meeting with Mancini. They had been methodical in their approach, ensuring that they did not reveal their suspicions too early. In the quiet of his modest office at the church, they began questioning him about his whereabouts on the nights of some of the recent assaults. The questions were straightforward, almost routine. Initially, Mancini was cooperative, his demeanor calm and patient as he answered the detectives' inquiries. However, as the conversation went on, his answers became more guarded, and his body language shifted. His hands, once folded neatly in front of him, began to twitch with agitation.

As they pressed him further, trying to nail down his whereabouts during the times of the attacks, it became clear that Mancini was growing uncomfortable. Unlike a regular priest, whose schedule might be easier to trace through church events and mass times, a deacon like Mancini led a life that was more like that of a regular fellow parishioner. He had a family, a private life that was harder to track. Baptiste knew that the alibis of men like Mancini were often more fluid, more difficult to pin down, especially when they didn't have the same level of oversight that an actual priest would have. Mancini seemed to take offense at the lengthy questioning, and the detectives could feel the tension rise in the small room.

The polite, cooperative man they had been speaking to moments ago turned slightly cold and defensive. His voice hardened, and his gaze sharpened as he leaned forward in his chair.

"How dare you accuse me of being involved in such heinous acts?" he spat. "I've dedicated my life to this community. I've given everything to these people, and now you come here, questioning me like I'm some kind of criminal? Betraying me and the church? After all I've done, this is how you repay me?"

Baptiste and Foret exchanged brief glances. They could tell that the once-friendly facade was cracking. Mancini's defensiveness was growing, and he seemed genuinely appalled that he was even a suspect in such a high-profile case. He became increasingly hostile, denying any involvement in the assaults and brushing off their questions as an insult to his character. His anger only seemed to escalate as they pressed him for more information, and it quickly became apparent that he would not be of any help. The meeting ended with Mancini standing up abruptly and dismissing them without a second thought.

Despite the deacon's refusal to cooperate fully, the detectives remained undeterred. They knew the case was far from over. As they left the church, they continued to discuss their next steps, knowing that even if Mancini had shut them down for now, they still needed to gather more evidence. They had to build a more detailed timeline, and piece together every shred of information they could find. They were determined to follow the trail, hoping to uncover something that would link the deacon to the series of tragic events. It was a slow process, but Baptiste and Foret knew they had to stay focused. The Phantom was still out there, and every moment counted.

In a bit of a surprise, the detectives discover that Mancini has a past criminal record, a history of violence that no one had previously considered. A thorough background check revealed that

## CHAPTER 3: DEVILISH DEACON?

many years ago, the now-scrutinized deacon had been arrested for separate assaults. The first incident, which had been buried deep in the archives, occurred when Mancini was in his twenties, a time when he was struggling with anger issues and a volatile temper. According to the police reports from that time, Mancini had been involved in a violent altercation at a local bar, where he had brutally attacked another man in what appeared to be a drunken rage. The charges were eventually dropped after the victim failed to press charges, but the arrest record remained, tucked away in the dusty corners of his past. The other incident happened a few years later when he was cited for damaging someone's property after a small confrontation at a grocery store. This charge was downgraded to a misdemeanor, and a few hours of community service was all he got.

These revelations raised red flags immediately for the investigators. While Mancini had long been seen as a pillar of the community, this new information cast a shadow over his otherwise pristine reputation. Baptiste and Foret knew that even a small history of violence was not something to be ignored, especially given the nature of the crimes they were investigating. The idea of a man of God, a deacon, no less having a checkered past was unsettling. And yet, it seemed to fit in an eerily disturbing way.

Looking more closely at Mancini's past, they couldn't help but draw parallels between his younger, more volatile self and the Phantom's current actions. The deacon's fiery sermons, his moral absolutism, and his disdain for those he deemed "sinners" were all consistent with the profile they had built of the elusive attacker. Mancini's calm composed demeanor in public seemed to mask something darker underneath, something capable of immense violence. Was it possible that the same man who had lashed out in a fit of rage years ago had now channeled that same anger into a more calculated form of vengeance? The thought made the detectives uneasy, but it also made him an even more viable suspect. The dots were starting to connect, and they couldn't ignore the mounting evidence and similarities that suggested Mancini might not just be a witness or a bystander in this case, he could very well be one of the leaders of the community moonlighting as the Phantom himself.

The investigation had taken an odd turn, and with each new piece of information, the lines between suspect and perpetrator were beginning to blot. Now, Mancini's calm and measured public persona seemed more like a mask—one that hid the dangerous impulses lurking just beneath the surface. Especially with the way Mancini ended their meeting and aggressively escorted the detectives out of his office. The detectives knew they had to tread carefully; the stakes had just been raised, and they were beginning to understand that the city could be dealing with a far more dangerous individual than they initially imagined.

As they continued their deep dive into Mancini's actions, and whereabouts on certain dates, Baptiste and Foret noticed a slight pattern. The vigilante's attacks usually seemed to occur after Mancini had delivered a particularly fiery sermon. *Could it be possible that Mancini was the Phantom, using his religious rhetoric as a justification for his violent acts? Or was this just a small coincidence, being it wasn't a very strong pattern? Could it be that even if Mancini was not the infamous Phantom, he could very well still unknowingly be stoking the attacker's inner fire by just being a normal attendee of the deacon's anxious homilies.* They needed to intensify their surveillance of Mancini, and it needed to happen immediately. They followed him everywhere he went, hoping he would slip up – or to even catch him in the act. But Mancini was elusive and, just like the Phantom, seemed to be one step ahead of them.

Their faces etched with fatigue and doubt, the detectives and their team were beginning to question the very foundation of their investigation. Days began to turn into weeks, as the elusive Phantom, the city's enigmatic vigilante, remained as slippery as ever. The initial theories, once a beacon of hope, were now dimming, casting a pall of uncertainty over the entire force.

As despair continued to creep into their hearts, a chilling additional chapter unfolded in the city's grim tale. A young man, his life nearly extinguished with brutal efficiency, was discovered in a desolate alleyway. His body, a grotesque testament to the Phantom's wrath, bore the unmistakable marks of a calculated, almost surgical, precision. His right hand and lower left leg, both severed with chilling accuracy, lay nearby, another reminder of the vigilante's relentless pursuit of justice, or perhaps, vengeance.

The victim, a known petty criminal, had confessed to mugging an elderly man earlier that evening. The police, ever vigilant in their pursuit of truth, believed that the Phantom had once again taken the law into his own hands, punishing the guilty man with a ferocity that defied comprehension. As the city trembled under the weight of this new horror, the detectives were forced to confront a stark reality: the Phantom's reign of terror was far from over and was now seemingly growing even harsher.

As the department delved deeper into the gruesome details of the latest crime. A perplexing question arose: Why had the Phantom chosen to amputate the victim's lower leg and hand? Why two limbs this time? They needed to question 'the victim' once again. So, when they pressed further, the wounded mugger confessed to a horrifying detail: during the robbery, he had repeatedly and needlessly kicked the elderly man while he lay helpless on the ground crying for him to stop.

Being a seasoned investigator, Foret offered a chilling insight. "That had to be why his lower leg was removed as well," he mused, connecting the dots between the mugger's cruelty and the Phantom's exact punishment. This revelation marked yet another layer in the tedious investigation. It implied that the Phantom must have actually witnessed this act of brutality firsthand, perhaps even while stalking the victim, to inflict such exact and specific retribution.

Baptiste, eager to exploit this new lead, proposed a thorough course of action. "Check every camera angle available in the area of this attack," she urged. "See if Mancini or anyone else was stalking the victim during that time frame."

The team, invigorated by this fresh perspective, redoubled their efforts, hoping to uncover the identity of the mysterious figure who was shaping the city's destiny, one gruesome act at a time. This was a chilling escalation in the Phantom's reign of terror. Until this point, no victim had suffered the loss of two limbs or body parts in a single attack. The severity of this latest crime sent shockwaves through the city yet again, leaving the detectives baffled as usual, and the public continually terrified. The brutality of the act suggested a level of calculated cruelty that surpassed even the most heinous of the Phantom's previous crimes. The young man was lucky to be alive, but he would now be heading to jail while accepting his new handicapped way of life.

The media, ever hungry for sensational news, seized upon this opportunity to fuel public fear and hysteria. A rookie officer, eager to impress, inadvertently leaked details of the gruesome crime to a local news outlet. The now-public information spread like wildfire, igniting a frenzy of speculation and conjecture. The city was gripped by a fresh wave of panic as citizens feared even more for their safety. The Phantom had truly become the most terrifying specter haunting the streets of the whole city. Even the usual criminals were laying low to avoid his vindicating rapture, which led to even less people on the streets.

The brutal attack on the latest victim, coupled with the new file they had built on Mancini, had breathed fresh life into the stalled investigation. For a while, the whole team had felt a surge of optimism. With each new piece of evidence that seemed to point toward Mancini, the sense of momentum had been undeniable. It was as if they were finally closing in on their elusive target. The case, which had once felt like a dead end, suddenly seemed full of possibility. Detectives and officers alike shared renewed energy, exchanging theories and ideas, and huddling over their next steps with newfound urgency. The air in the department had shifted, from frustration to something akin to hope.

But unfortunately, that new hope was short-lived. As the days passed, the team's confidence began to falter again. After reviewing more of the good-quality camera footage from the area where the latest assault occurred, they discovered a key detail that would unravel their entire case against Deacon Mancini. The time stamps on the footage confirmed something they hadn't noticed before: At the precise moments the newest victim had been attacked, Mancini had been in police custody, being questioned by detectives at the precinct. It was an undeniable alibi. The assault, horrifying as it was, could not have been his doing. Mancini, once the prime suspect, was quickly crossed off the top of the list.

It was a painful setback, especially after all the work that had gone into building a case against him. The team, once boosted by the possibility that they had finally found their man, now felt deflated. There was an inevitable sense of disappointment as the investigation veered off course. But the truth was, they couldn't afford to sit back in defeat. While Mancini had been exonerated as the perpetrator, the case was far from over. Some felt that even though he might not be the acting Phantom, there was still a possibility that the famed assailant could still be a regular at Mancini's sermons. The deacon could even be pulling the strings from behind the scenes, while a devout follower of his was doing the actual dirty deeds. The detectives agreed that the best course of action was to continue monitoring Mancini, but now with a different angle. They would focus less on him and more on the people he interacted with regularly, particularly his parishioners. His position as a church leader meant that he had a community of followers who looked up to him, and one of them could still be their perpetrator.

The team was wary of dismissing Mancini entirely. After all, just because he wasn't the direct attacker didn't mean he couldn't somehow still be involved. It wasn't beyond the realm of possibility that one of his impressionable, perhaps troubled, parishioners might have been influenced by him purposely or even accidentally through his heated sermons. The church itself became the next focal point of their surveillance. Officers were tasked with keeping a low profile around the congregation, hoping that someone from within might slip up, or that a hidden lead would emerge. The possibility that Mancini was connected to the case through a proxy was still on the table, and the team could not afford to let their guard down. The investigation, as disheartening as the setback was, had to march on. The truth was still out there but finding it would require a different path forward.

## CHAPTER 3: DEVILISH DEACON?

The media storm surrounding the case grew even more intense. The high-profile coverage of the case had captured the public's attention like few others in recent memory. News outlets were broadcasting every twist and turn, each new development adding fuel to the fire of an increasingly polarized public opinion. With the interviews airing on TV, there was an unsettling shift in tone. While the mugging of an elderly man, especially the one involving the now double amputee, would typically evoke universal outrage, some locals were not only indifferent but were again actually supportive of the Phantom's actions. In fact, a growing portion of residents had openly begun to rally behind the vigilante, openly expressing their admiration for the brutal acts he had carried out.

This latest story became something of a symbol for those disillusioned with the less than stellar justice system. These "fans" of the Phantom, as the media had dubbed them, saw his violent attacks not as crimes, but as acts of necessary retribution. In their eyes, the Phantom wasn't a criminal, he was an antihero, a ruthless agent of justice in a city they viewed as overrun by crime and corruption. The police, in their eyes, had long since lost the trust of the people. Crime rates were soaring up to this point, the officers were seen as ineffective, and the scandals within the department were well documented. The Phantom, in contrast, was taking matters into his own hands, doing what the police could not, or would not do. To these supporters, his bloody methods were mostly justified. The local news anchors, who dutifully reported the crimes in a traditional, usually neutral tone, were taken aback by the growing public support for the Phantom. During interviews with some of his vocal supporters, the anchors were visibly shocked, struggling to hide their astonishment as the so-called "victims" of the Phantom's violence, were vilified in favor of the vigilante. One particularly heated interview featured a man who, when asked about the double-amputee that mugged the elderly man, responded coldly: "That guy probably had it coming. Maybe the Phantom's just doing what the police should have been doing all along." The anchors were left sputtering, trying to bring the conversation back to the tragic nature of the crime, but the supporters' sentiments echoed a truth they hadn't expected. There was a deep undercurrent of frustration within the community, a perceivable distrust in the justice system that had only been exacerbated by years of perceived failure.

As more of these interviews aired, the contrast between the anchors' astonishment and the unwavering support for the Phantom became impossible to ignore. In some circles, the media coverage itself had inadvertently fueled the Phantom's growing legend. The more the police were portrayed as inept or corrupt, the more the Phantom was viewed as a new symbol of the people's frustration with the system. Even those who would never resort to violence in their own lives were beginning to see his actions in a more sympathetic light. The line between right and wrong, justice and vengeance, was blurring in the eyes of many. Some simply felt that he was cleaning up the streets, taking out the trash that the police had failed to address. It was a dangerous and unsettling mindset, but it was gaining traction.

For the city, this shift in public opinion was a major blow to the authorities. The police were now faced with the uncomfortable reality that their inability to control crime had inadvertently created a new kind of vigilante antihero. The Phantom, with his brutal methods and undeniable effectiveness, had become a figure of both fear and admiration. It wasn't just a case of criminal activity—it reflected the people's eroding trust in the very institutions that were supposed to protect them. The more the Phantom's supporters praised him, the more complicated the situation became for the police. Every new interview with a fan of his only added fuel to the fire, turning what should have been a straightforward case of crime and punishment into something far more complex: a battle for the soul of the city itself.

The situation quickly escalated into an ethical battleground that divided the very fabric of the community. The growing public support for the Phantom and the violent acts he was committing had sparked an intense moral dispute among the locals, and the police department knew they had to act fast to prevent it from spiraling further out of control. If this division wasn't quelled soon, it threatened to become another festering issue that the already-struggling city simply could not afford. The department's priority was no longer just about catching the Phantom, it was about maintaining order, restoring faith in law enforcement, and preventing this vigilante movement from becoming an unmanageable force.

For the archdiocese, the situation was equally delicate. The church, once a respected institution in the Crescent City, now found itself under intense scrutiny due to its perceived association with the Phantom. The growing speculation that the Phantom was linked to the church, or that some of his followers were parishioners, had placed the archdiocese at the center of a storm. The scandal was compounded by the fact that, for many, the church's position on morality and justice was now being questioned in the most public of ways. What had once been routine topics of debate, the weak economy and the ongoing controversies surrounding crooked city officials—were now being overshadowed by this new, more fiery issue. The church had always been a pillar of moral guidance for many in the city, but now that very foundation was shaking. People were starting to ask a lot of questions. Wondering if the church had turned a blind eye to the violence or if, perhaps, it had even played a role in nurturing the Phantom's twisted sense of perceived justice.

Even the state government, which had been preoccupied with its own political issues, could no longer ignore the growing unrest. The Louisiana Governor, once focused on the usual political debates and the ongoing scandals plaguing local officials, now found himself watching the case with growing concern. It wasn't just the question of catching the Phantom that worried him, it was the bigger question of what would happen if this vigilante violence continued to escalate. Would the city's fragile peace be shattered by more public support for the Phantom's actions? Would the police and local officials be able to restore order before it was too late? The idea of the National Guard being called in to assist with the situation was becoming more of a reality every day. The Governor now found himself grappling with the tough decision of whether the Guard would be needed to help track down the Phantom or to intervene in the public's growing civil unrest. The people of the Crescent City were becoming deeply divided—many now saw the Phantom as a symbol of tough justice, while others viewed him as nothing more than a dangerous fanatical criminal who needed to be stopped at all costs.

The situation was rapidly evolving from a simple law enforcement issue into something far more complex. The public's increasing polarization over the Phantom's actions had ignited heated debates about justice, punishment, and the role of the state in maintaining order. On one hand, there were those who believed that the Phantom was a necessary evil, cleaning up a broken and corrupt system. On the other hand, there were those who saw him as a threat to the very makeup of society, a lawless vigilante who needed to be brought to justice before his actions spun further out of control. The moral dilemma was becoming more and more pronounced, with residents arguing over whether the Phantom's actions were a form of justice or simply a dangerous precedent for anarchy.

Meanwhile, the police were caught in the middle of this growing conflict. The department was faced not only with the difficult task of apprehending the Phantom but also with the challenge of trying to restore a sense of order in a city that was increasingly divided over his actions. Public opinion was now an important battleground. The police had to walk a fine line. While they needed to pursue the Phantom aggressively to maintain law and order, they also had to be mindful of the fact that a significant portion of the population had begun cheering him on. The department understood that any misstep could make the situation even worse, turning public opinion into full-scale civil unrest.

Governor Chisham, for his part, had to be the voice of reason and order, assuring the people of Louisiana that the situation would be handled with care. He had to prepare for the worst-case scenario—where reserve troops would be needed to intervene, if that option became inevitable. It was a difficult balancing act, and one that would require careful navigation of both political and social tensions. His primary duty now was to assist the mayor any way possible to keep the city from descending into chaos. *Would sending troops ultimately make things better or worse?* The stakes grew higher daily, and the solution seemed further out of reach.

# CHAPTER 4: REACQUAINTANCE

As anonymous crimes followed by their vindictive assaults continued, the City of New Orleans, once united—even if only by fear—was now completely divided on the morality issues of the Phantom case. The city grappled with questions about justice, vengeance, and the darker sides of human nature. What had driven the Phantom to commit such horrific acts? Was it strictly vengeance in the name of God, or was there something even more sinister lurking behind his motives? Or was it truly just for his enjoyment, a wicked hobby that he had grown to love, all while using the church as an excuse to "save" these sinful people? The NOPD had worked tirelessly to unravel the great mystery. Was the Phantom's motive truly a religious vindication, or was it merely an elaborate facade for a much deeper, more disturbing pastime? Many questioned whether he truly believed he was chosen by God to punish sinners and to save their souls, while others thought he was in fact carrying out God's work.

## CHAPTER 4: REACQUAINTANCE

This religious fanatic had begun to see himself as a modern-day spiritualist, a figure of grayness spreading his confused and warped message of retribution and vindication. As Baptiste delved deeper into this madman's psyche, she began to accept more probable unsettling motivations behind his actions. It became clear that the Phantom was not just a man of twisted beliefs, but also consumed by a desperate thirst for power and control. In his mind, by punishing sinners, he was saving their souls in the long-run and restoring order to a chaotic world. A world he saw as teetering on the edge of collapse. In his eyes, he was not the monster they reported him to be, but a savior, desperately trying to bring balance to a world he believed had lost its way. The pain and injuries now-were temporary, whereas Gehenna, was eternal.

Ricardo Lopez, now wearing an eye patch over his right eye from the previous ambush, moved through the streets with a heightened sense of unease. The scar from that attack still throbbed, a constant reminder of the danger that had nearly cost him his life. Yet, despite his vigilance, he couldn't shake the feeling that his past assailant was still watching, still hunting him. He hadn't been sleeping well lately, and Ricardo needed to let loose. He had been cooped up, hiding in his home ever since that fateful night.

This time though, Lopez wasn't alone. He was with a young and attractive prostitute; someone he had sought out for the night. But even in the midst of his present indulgence, he couldn't ignore the creeping sense of danger. This tormenting sense had consumed his life, but he had to overcome it if he was going to ever have any semblance of the normal life he had prior to their untimely meeting. He figured that ominous figure from his past—his attacker—was somewhere nearby, stalking them both. But he had to put it behind him. He now carried a switchblade knife and pepper spray in his pocket, just in case. He would be more prepared if their paths ever crossed again. Although he wasn't aware, this occasion wasn't just about him being targeted anymore; the threat had now extended to his lady companion as well. The ominous nightmare of the past had come back to haunt him, and just like before, there was nowhere to hide.

The air was poignant with the scent of cheap perfume and stale cigarette smoke as Lopez and his companion indulged in their illicit pleasure. He moved slightly awkward, but as the shot of bourbon went down, his constant uneasiness slowly faded. Lost in the moment, neither noticed the encroaching darkness, the silent figure that had slipped into their squalid motel room.

His right eye was still clouded by the aftermath of their last encounter; he was oblivious to the familiar danger that now lurked in the gloom of the barely lit room. His labored breaths and her occasional panting were the only sounds that filled the dingy cramped space. Suddenly, an intense pain exploded in his temple, and he was sent tumbling from the bed onto the cold, unforgiving floor. A blood-curdling scream pierced the silence but was quickly stifled. Before Lopez could react, another blow landed, and his vision began to blur. As consciousness faded, he heard a familiar, chilling voice echoing in the darkness.

"You still haven't learned your lesson, Ricardo? I will not fail you or our Father, and I will do my best to save you from Gehenna once again." The words hung in the air, a chilling reminder of the relentless pursuit that had consumed his life.

Lopez's eyelids fluttered open, a groggy haze clouding his vision. A sharp, throbbing pain pulsed in the side of his head, a stark reminder of the quick and brutal attack. As his senses slowly returned, he heard a woman's mournful cries, a sound that sent a

## CHAPTER 4: REACQUAINTANCE

shiver down his spine. With a groan, he forced himself to sit up, his eyes scanning the blood-soaked bed. The once-familiar motel room was now a scene of carnage, a testament to the violence that had unfolded. A wave of nausea washed over him as he noticed the crimson stain that marred the sheets.

A cold dread settled in his gut as he began to realize the extent of the horror. His gaze fell upon his left hand, where he clutched a horrifying sight: his own severed member, still pulsing with life. A guttural cry escaped his lips as he brought the mutilated appendage closer to his face, the full extent of the depravity dawning upon him. In a desperate attempt to alleviate the new excruciating pain, he reached down to examine the wound. A fresh wave of agony shot through him, causing him to double over in pain. The woman's cries also grew louder, a haunting melody of suffering that echoed through the room.

As he lay there, bleeding and broken, a chilling realization struck him: if he were to survive this ordeal, he would need to absolutely change his ways. The once-fearless man was now a shell of his former self, a victim of a twisted game of cat and mouse. The woman stirred, a sharp pain shooting through her chest. Her vision blurred as she tried to focus on the horror before her. Her left breast was missing, a gaping wound oozing blood. A cold dread seized her as she realized the extent of her mutilation, as well as his.

A knock echoed through the room, interrupting the brief silence. "Is everything alright in there?" a voice called out. Neither Lopez nor the woman responded, their bodies ravaged, and their spirits broken. All they could do was mourn in pain together in an eerie duet. The door eventually creaked open, and a concerned neighbor stepped into the gruesome scene. Shock and horror etched his face as he took in the carnage. Summoning his courage, the fellow patron dialed 911, his voice trembling as he relayed the horrific incident.

Paramedics quickly arrived, swiftly assessing the situation. Lopez, though severely injured, was still alive. The woman, however, was clinging to life, her blood loss critical. Sadly, despite the best efforts of the medical team, the woman in the end, succumbed to her gory injury, becoming the first confirmed homicide of the Phantom's twisted agenda. Her untimely death is sure to send shockwaves through the fragile community, a stark reminder of the terror that lurks, hidden in this once festive city.

The very-publicized death of the streetwalker did indeed jolt the inhabitants of the area. News outlets couldn't get enough of the story, and the gruesome details spread quickly through the streets. The Phantom, now also being referred to by some as "The Vindicator" had crossed a terrifying line. What had once been seen as a series of isolated, cryptic attacks was now undeniable: this killer was becoming bolder, more reckless, and even more brutal. The city was paralyzed by even greater fear, as its citizens were unsure of where the next strike would come. Some of his new troves of fans slowly stepped back to re-analyze their true feelings of the man they had actually been defending.

As the increased hysteria spread, the pressure on the NOPD to catch this newly minted killer, intensified. Citizens clamored for answers, and the police were left scrambling for clues as per the norm. But in truth, the investigation had made little progress. Without security cameras in the dive motel where the assault and murder had occurred, there was no footage, no clear evidence, and no real leads to follow up on. The woman was a working regular at the motel, so she had the room under her name for a dirt-cheap rate. This Vindicator's identity remained elusive as ever, a figure

## CHAPTER 4: REACQUAINTANCE

that could seemingly slip through the cracks at will.

Even Ricardo Lopez, now the first repeat victim of the Phantom, was no closer to identifying his old acquaintance. Despite the familiarity of the attacker's presence, Lopez's mind remained clouded with confusion. The haunting voice, the eerie sense of being hunted—it all felt like a nightmare he once again couldn't escape. But even with the fear and the pain, he could not help but sense a deeper connection to the man behind the mask. Yet, no matter how hard he tried, the answers eluded him.

As the weeks dragged on, the city's fear only grew. The Phantom—or Vindicator—had become an enigma, a figure of terror who operated with impunity. People whispered his names throughout the day, casting nervous glances over their shoulders, wondering if they, too, might become his next target. The gruesome murder of the streetwalker, even if unintentional, had made it impossible for anyone to deny the killer's existence any longer. What had once been tempered speculation that he at least was not a killer, now felt like a living, breathing entity stalking the streets for his prey.

The pressure on the police force had reached a boiling point. Police Commissioner Francisco was under fire from all sides—his officers were running out of leads, and public confidence was rapidly eroding. Every day brought new reports, new sightings, but all of them were vague, and none of them were concrete enough to lead to a breakthrough. The case was growing cold, the scent of failure heavy in the air, and Baptiste couldn't help but wonder if they were missing something crucial, something right in front of them.

Meanwhile, the castrated Lopez found himself trapped in his own private hell. The attacks had left him forever physically scarred, but it was the emotional toll that was even more crushing.

Each time he closed his eyes, he could still hear the Phantom's voice, and the weight of those haunting words. He had tried to push the memories away, but the specter of his old acquaintance lingered. It wasn't just the brutality of the attacks that haunted him, it was the strange, twisted sense of purpose that the Phantom seemed to have.

*Could he have known him? Could they have crossed paths before in a different life, before all this madness?* His mind raced with fragments of old memories, faces, and places that now felt distant, like pieces of a puzzle that no longer fit. He couldn't help but feel that somehow, the key to understanding this whole misery lay hidden in his past. *But what was it? And why couldn't he remember?*

Baptiste and her team were devastated when they heard about the prostitute's death. The news hit them hard, not just because of the tragedy itself, but because they knew it would have far-reaching consequences. The murder had just escalated everything. The pressure on the department to solve this case would now be more intense than ever. What had once been a series of disturbing events was now an even higher-profile murder investigation, and the public's demand for answers was growing by the hour.

With the stakes high, tensions within the police department began to rise. The weight of the case—and the public's growing demands for justice—was pushing everyone to their breaking points. The Homicide Unit, already stretched thin with forced budget cuts, found themselves at odds with Team Baptiste and Foret, who were more focused on solving the Phantom case than managing routine investigations. Homicide was itching to take over control of the investigation now that a fatality had incurred. The pressure was beginning to fracture their once-cohesive teamwork.

The division between the two groups became profound, with

every encounter between the units feeling charged and uneasy. There were heated arguments over jurisdiction, disagreements over how the investigation should be handled, and accusations of miscommunication. Some officers in the Homicide Unit felt that Baptiste and Foret were hogging resources and taking too long to make progress, while Baptiste's team felt the Homicide Unit was obstructive, more concerned with their new opportunity to prop up their own reputations by getting credit for finally solving the high-profile case.

Tension continued to build, and what had begun as a professional disagreement began to look more like an open feud. There were whispers in the hallways, cold glares in the break room, and subtle sabotages of each other's work. The in-fighting only made things more difficult, especially as both teams faced mounting pressure from above. The brass in City Hall was demanding results, and the pressure to deliver a breakthrough was relentless. At the same time, the city's residents grew more and more fearful, watching every news update with anxiety, wondering if they would be safe in their own neighborhoods ever again.

For Baptiste and Foret, the stress of trying to solve the case while navigating the growing division between their own colleagues felt like walking a tightrope. They knew that any misstep could unravel the fragile trust they had left within their team. The cracks in the department were showing, and the killer seemed to be feeding off the discord. With every new obstacle—both internal and external—the investigation seemed to slip further from their grasp. The pressure was suffocating, and no one seemed to have an answer to when it would all end. The detectives had been working countless hours as usual, pushing themselves beyond the limits of exhaustion. The case seemed never-ending, and with each new lead that went nowhere, their frustration only grew. The constant sense of dread and uncertainty was beginning to wear them thin. Their nerves were frayed, with their tempers shorter than usual. Every day felt like a battle, and neither of them knew how much longer they could keep going at this pace. The weight of the case was starting to seep into Baptiste and Foret's personal lives, and they both began to feel the emotional toll it was taking. What had once been an intense but manageable workload was now all-consuming. Long hours at the office, endless nights of peering over recorded surveillance, and the constant pressure of trying to solve a case that seemed to be slipping further from their grasp, began to erode their energy and patience. The stresses of the investigation had crept into every corner of their lives, leaving little room for anything else. They found themselves increasingly irritable and withdrawn. The exhaustion from working around the clock had worn them down physically, but it was the emotional toll that was truly beginning to take over. They snapped at colleagues and each other, struggled to focus during briefings, and often felt on edge, as if the ever-present sense of impending danger was seeping into their very bones. Even simple things like taking a moment to relax or enjoy a quiet meal had become distant luxuries. They barely had time for themselves anymore, let alone for the people who mattered most. Relationships, both personal and professional, began to fray as they became consumed by the case. The calls to family members grew shorter, the time spent with loved ones became almost nonexistent. What had once been a life they could balance between work and personal connections was now dominated by the dark weight of the investigation.

And in the back of their minds, there was always the nagging question—one that grew more pressing with each passing day:

## CHAPTER 4: REACQUAINTANCE

*Would they ever catch the vindictive Phantom, or would he slip away again, and again, leaving only annihilation in his wake?* The haunting uncertainty of that question became a constant companion, pushing them forward, even as it drained them. It was the only thing that kept them going, even when it seemed like the case was slipping further into the dark.

After one of their long, grueling days at work, Pete decided to invite Zoe over to his place for a few beers. The exhaustion from another day on the case wore heavy on both of them, and Pete figured it might be a good opportunity to unwind. At first, Zoe declined, citing how tired she was and how much work she still had to do. But Pete, sensing she needed a break as much as he did, pressed her a little more. After some playful persuasion and a couple of jokes to lighten the mood, Zoe finally relented, agreeing to stop by for just a short while.

Though their professional lives had always been closely intertwined, their personal dynamic was a different story. Pete and Zoe had been romantically linked on two previous occasions, brief encounters that never really went anywhere. Both times, the relationship fizzled out quickly, with Zoe always pulling back before anything serious could develop. She had made it clear from the beginning that she wanted to keep things strictly professional, especially given how well they worked together in the field.

But Pete had been wanting more for some time now. He had always thought there was more to their relationship than just camaraderie. The chemistry between them was undeniable, and it seemed to him like there was an unspoken tension lingering beneath the surface. Yet, despite his persistent efforts, Zoe had always managed to keep him at a friendly distance. No matter how much he pushed, she never seemed willing to cross that line again.

Still, tonight, there was a flicker of hope in Pete's mind. Maybe tonight would be different.

Zoe arrived at Pete's place a little after seven, with a bag of snacks in hand. They were both eager to relax for a change, and tonight was the perfect opportunity. The Saints game was on, and it had been a long time since they had any downtime. With the case weighing heavily on both of them, they needed a break more than ever. Zoe had brought chips, some dip, and a couple of pizzas, knowing Pete wouldn't think of all the small details. She smiled as she walked through the door, glad to be out of the office and away from the constant pressure.

They settled onto Pete's couch, each grabbing a drink—Pete with a beer, Zoe with a glass of wine. The familiar comfort of the room, the low hum of the TV, and the casual atmosphere made the weight of the world feel a little lighter. They hadn't had much time to relax together recently, and Zoe could already feel the tension on her shoulders starting to ease. It was the kind of night they both needed, away from the chaos and stress of their jobs.

As the game started, they leaned back, sipping their drinks and occasionally cheering or groaning at the plays onscreen. But even as the game unfolded before them, the case they were working on lingered in the background, a distraction neither of them could completely shake. Every now and then, one of them would mention something work-related—a suspect, a lead, a piece of evidence—but both tried to steer the conversation away from the case as much as they could. They didn't want tonight to be consumed by work; they needed a few hours of peace. For those moments, the world outside Pete's living room seemed to slow down, and they let themselves simply enjoy the game and each other's company. The case would still be there tomorrow, but for now, they both tried to keep it at bay, savoring the rare opportunity to unwind and just be themselves for a short while.

Pete couldn't resist anymore. The scent of her perfume was intoxicating, a mix of vanilla and jasmine that seemed to cling to the air around them. That, along with her natural beauty, made everything else fade into the background. He had been trying to keep his distance, to maintain the line between friendship and something more, but tonight it all felt impossible to ignore. He leaned in closer, his hand moving to her shoulders, gently massaging the tense muscles there. The touch was comforting, almost instinctive, and without thinking, he pressed his lips to her neck.

Zoe was initially surprised, her body stiffening for a moment, but she didn't push him away immediately. The unexpected kiss sent a ripple of warmth through her, a warmth she hadn't felt in a long time. For a few moments, as they kissed, everything seemed to fall into place. The chaos of the case, the stress, the constant pressure—it all melted away, leaving only the two of them in the quiet comfort of Pete's living room. In those brief moments, it felt like nothing else mattered.

But as the kiss deepened, something inside Zoe shifted. The fog of desire began to clear, and she realized what was happening. The weight of their professional relationship, the boundaries they had carefully built, crashed back into her mind. She pulled away abruptly, her breath shallow, her heart racing.

"We can't, Pete," she said, her voice shaky but firm. "We're betraying our professional ethics, and I can't allow myself to get involved with a co-worker again. I told you this before—I don't want to lose you as a friend or a partner. It would kill me."

Pete froze, still close to Zoe's lips, disappointment in his eyes, but he didn't push her further. He understood. What else could he do? He had hoped, in some corner of his heart, that tonight might be different, but he knew how much Zoe valued their professional boundaries. She was a dedicated detective, and he respected that, even if it stung. Neither of them could afford to jeopardize their careers, especially not for something as uncertain as a relationship that had already been complicated by the tension of their previous hook-ups.

Zoe gathered her things, feeling the weight of the decision pressing on her chest. As she left his home, she couldn't shake the feeling that something had shifted between them—something that couldn't be undone. She knew she had made the right choice, but a pang of sadness lingered in her chest, tugging at her heart. She had walked away from something that might have been good, something that might have been worth pursuing. But was it the right choice? She wasn't so sure. She tried to focus on the decision she had made, convincing herself it was the only one that made sense. But deep down, there was a nagging thought—*what if she was missing out on something? What if they could have been happy together?* The uncertainty lingered, making her question if she had made the right decision after all.

Zoe drove through the dimly lit streets, the steady hum of her car did little to quiet the storm inside her. The night air felt heavy, even though the windows were rolled up, and her mind raced with conflicting thoughts. She glanced in the rearview mirror, as if searching for some sign, some clarity, but there was nothing. Just the dark stretch of road behind her, and the thoughts of her own doubts creeping forward. She couldn't shake the feeling of guilt that clung to her. Had she been too harsh with Pete? He had made it clear how he felt, and yet she had shut him down again without much hesitation. She had done it out of a sense of duty, a belief that

## CHAPTER 4: REACQUAINTANCE

maintaining their professional integrity was the only way forward. But now, as the minutes passed, she wondered if she had overreacted. Pete had been nothing but supportive, and their connection was undeniable. Maybe, just maybe, she had been too afraid to take that next step, to allow herself to experience something real outside of the job. The way he kissed her—so tender, yet full of longing, kept replaying in her mind. It was as if he had waited for the right moment, but Zoe had pulled away before they could even see where it might go. The warmth of his touch, the softness of his lips on her skin, still lingered, making her feel a strange emptiness that she hadn't expected. She had told him she didn't want to lose him, but was that true? Or was she just too afraid of what their relationship might become? Too afraid of what it could cost them both. She shook her head, trying to push the thoughts aside. *This was what she had chosen, right?* She couldn't afford to get caught up in something that would distract her from the work that mattered most. They were partners, first and foremost. Their connection had always been professional, and she had always respected that. She needed to keep her focus on the case, on the job that demanded so much of her. That was her responsibility. That was what kept her grounded.

As she arrived home, the quiet ache in her chest still hadn't gone away. She wasn't sure what she was mourning—whether it was the relationship she let slip through her fingers yet again, or the part of herself that had chosen duty over desire. Maybe it was both. Maybe she was just tired of feeling like she had to choose between the two, tired of walking a line so thin that every step seemed to bring her closer to falling off.

# CHAPTER 5: FORGIVE ME FATHER, FOR I HAVE SINNED

The vaunted Vindicator, a figure once cloaked in mystery and fear, found himself facing an unexpected challenge—a possible end to the very mission that had consumed his life. The streets that had once been his kingdom, a vast canvas upon which he painted his brand of justice, were no longer his alone. A surge in police activity had brought unwanted attention to the city's underbelly, and the public, once terrified of him, now sought to catch a glimpse of the so-called anti-hero. News outlets broadcast reports of his exploits, and rumors of his presence spread like wildfire. No longer could he operate with the secrecy and swiftness that had once defined him. Every shadow was a potential witness, every corner a trap waiting to be sprung. The very vigilance that had once granted him freedom of action had now become his greatest hindrance. The hunter was now the hunted.

For the first time in what seemed like ages, he found himself with more time on his hands. The streets, once so familiar and comforting in their solitude, had grown increasingly alien to him. Without his almost nightly crusades, his sense of purpose began to wither. He had never been one for introspection—his recent life had always been about action, about saving souls, and righting wrongs with swift, decisive force. But with the passage of time and the absence of his usual outlets, a strange stillness began to settle over him. The sanctuary he had built for himself, once a refuge from the chaos of the city, now became a prison for his mind.

Within the quiet, dim-lit confines of his apartment, he found himself confronting something far more insidious than any criminal he had ever faced, his own warped conscience. The overwhelming certainty that had guided his every move now seemed distant, like a fading memory. Guilt, a new feeling foreign to his typically righteous and unyielding mindset, began to creep in. He had always seen himself as a force for justice, and for the Lord, a necessary instrument of divine wrath in a city rife with sinners and corruption. He had justified his actions by telling himself that he was cleansing the world, saving the damned from hell, and punishing those who had escaped the consequences of their own wrongdoing. Yet, now, as he sat in the silence of his dark sanctuary, a growing sense of unease took root. Was he truly fulfilling God's will, or had he merely become another manifestation of vengeance, masked in righteousness?

The more he dwelled on this question, the more it gnawed at him. The certainty he had once held in his heart, that his cause was just and his actions righteous, seemed less clear in the light of his current isolation. He had always believed that his methods were justified—that the ends would always justify the means. But now, in the stillness of his mind, doubts slithered in. *Had his harsh methods, his often-brutal approach to justice, been the right course? Or had he, in his zeal to right wrongs, crossed a line that could never be undone?* The once black-and-white view of the world was now clouded with shades of grey, and the Phantom/Vindicator, the great arbiter of woeful justice, found himself for the first time, uncertain of the very path he had chosen.

This introspection was unlike anything he had ever experienced. It was a stark contrast to the vigilance that had fueled his mission in the past. He had been driven by a righteous indignation, a belief that his actions were divinely sanctioned. But as the recent days passed, he found himself questioning whether his actions had truly been for the greater good, or if they were simply the result of a man trying to impose his own sense of justice on a world that could not—or would not—bend to his will. The stillness of his shelter, once a refuge, now was a suffocating void, and he was forced to confront the reality that perhaps he had become as much a prisoner of his own creation as the criminal she had sought to reprove. Despite the countless souls he had purportedly redeemed in his mind, this fledgling nagging doubt persisted. If he was truly fulfilling God's divine will, was his brand of justice, born of vigilante fervor, truly aligned with the Lord's intended path? Though unplanned, he had taken a life. *Could, and would this be accepted by his master? Was he now just as bad as the people that he was tasked with helping?* A strange dichotomy emerged within him: a sense of pride mingled with profound remorse. He revealed in the significant impact he had on countless lives, yet a pang of guilt pierced his wounded heart. *Had his methods been a little too harsh, his judgments too swift?* His mind raced, grappling with these conflicting emotions. He was a tool of God's righteous wrath, accustomed to decisive strikes and quick retribution. But now, he found himself questioning the very nature of his existence. *Was he merely a man,*

## CHAPTER 5: FORGIVE ME FATHER, FOR I HAVE SINNED

*flawed and fallible, driven by a misguided sense of purpose?* He realized that his path had become increasingly convoluted. The line between justice and judgment clouded, the distinction between salvation and condemnation obscured. He was somewhat of a hero to some, a villain to others, and perhaps even a tragic figure caught in the crossfire of his own righteousness.

The grim news report echoed through the darkened apartment, a stark contrast to the quiet desperation within. His latest target, a young woman caught in the wrong place at the wrong time, had met an unfortunate and tragic end. He had intended to punish, but save her, just like all the others, a harsh lesson for her indiscretions. But his hand had slipped, his blade had cut too deep. A crude mastectomy, a punishment meant to humiliate and deter, had instead claimed her young life. The weight of her untimely death bore down upon him, a heavy burden that threatened to crush his once indestructible spirit. He was a man accustomed to delivering divine justice, but now found himself a victim of his own brutality. His heart, once hardened by a righteous cause, was now filled with remorse. He had failed, not just in his mission to purify the city, but also in the eyes of the Lord. The divine mandate he had embraced had led him down a dark and twisted path, one that had claimed an almost innocent life.

As he sat alone in the dim light, the echoes of his actions haunted him. The young woman's face, filled with terror and pain, flashed before his eyes. He had seen countless souls corrupted by sin, but this one, so young and vulnerable, had broken him. The weight of her death was a constant reminder of his own failures and mortality, a stark contrast to the immortal righteousness he had once strived for. He could no longer escape the haunting cost of his actions. The same shadows that once offered him relief now seemed to mock him, stretching long across the walls like dark tendrils creeping into his very soul. There was no longer the comforting hum of action to drown out the questions that clung to the air. His mind, once a razor-sharp instrument of justice, was now consumed with doubt and self-loathing. The line between justice and vengeance, once so clear in his eyes, had blurred into a murky, indistinguishable fog. He had crossed that line long ago, yet it was only now that he could truly comprehend the extent of his failed transgressions.

What had begun as a mission to purge the city of its evil had turned into something far darker. His methods had grown more extreme, his punishments more severe. He had justified each strike, each act of violence, by telling himself that it was for the greater good, that the end result—a city free from sin, and sinners saved, was worth the cost. The people he had harmed, the lives he had altered or destroyed, had become inescapable resonations. It no longer mattered whether he had been right in his cause; the fact remained that he had taken a life, and in doing so, he had become a replica of the very thing he had once fought against to save. His spiritual cause had twisted into something far less noble, and in this moment of profound reflection, he could see it clearly. His small living room felt oppressive, the walls closing in on him as the candle's flickering flame illuminated the dark recesses of his mind. It was as if the darkness of his own making had come to life, dancing on the walls and ceiling in mocking rhythm. There was no escape from it, no way to outrun the truth that had finally caught up to him. The very air felt heavy with the weight of his remorse.

He sat hunched over a small, cluttered table, a half-empty glass of crimson wine trembling in his hand. The liquid swirled slowly, his gaze distant and fixed on nothing in particular, as if he were

## CHAPTER 5: FORGIVE ME FATHER, FOR I HAVE SINNED

seeing something beyond the physical world. His once-righteous visage, the face that had been both feared and admired, was now etched with the marks of despair. Lines of worry and regret had settled into his features, the hard edges of his face softened by the weight of guilt. His jaw, which had once been set with unflinching determination, now trembled. His eyes, which had once burned with the conviction of his divine mission, were hollow, devoid of the fire that had once made him a force to be reckoned with. The man who had once been driven by an unshakable sense of purpose now found himself drowning in a sea of self-doubt and remorse. For the first time, he could not tell himself that he was doing God's work. He could no longer convince himself that his mission was justified, that every brutal act was necessary for the greater good. The mask he had worn to shield himself from the weight of his actions now felt like an imprisonment, an unshakable burden that trapped him in a cycle of guilt and torment. The world he had created, a world where he was both judge and executioner, had crumbled, and in its place was a man who now struggled to know what he stood for.

In his desperation, he had tried to numb the pain with alcohol, a fleeting escape from the constant barrage of guilt. But the wine did little to dull the sharp edges of his conscience. Each sip was a reminder that no amount of distraction could erase the reality of what he had become. He had crossed a line from which there was no return, and now, as the hours ticked by, the full weight of his actions crushed him. The man who had once moved through the city like a reaper of retribution, now saw himself as nothing more than a fallen angel—lost, broken, and almost irredeemable. He muted the TV and placed the glass down on the table, its contents swirling in a slow, dizzying motion, as though mirroring the turmoil inside him. The silence stretched out before him like an endless void. His body now seemed heavy and lifeless, as if all the energy that had once propelled him forward had been drained. The darkness that surrounded him was no longer something he could escape, nor did he want to. For the first time, he was forced to face himself, to confront the full extent of his sins without the comfort of justification or excuses. He sat there for what felt like an eternity, lost in the suffocating quiet of his own mind. He no longer had the answers he had so confidently believed in. The certainty that had once defined him—his unwavering belief in his mission—had been shattered. In its place was a profound emptiness, a sense of loss that was deeper than any physical wound he had ever inflicted. He was a man consumed, a tragic figure whose journey toward redemption now seemed as distant as the stars. He closed his eyes, feeling the weight of his guilt wash over him once more. In that moment, he realized that no amount of self-inflicted punishment, no act of vengeance or retribution, could ever undo the damage he had caused. The sins of the past would forever be with him, etched into the fabric of his soul. And yet, despite the overwhelming despair, a small part of him—though faint—whispered that perhaps redemption might still be possible. But whether he could ever truly escape the torment within was a question only time would answer. The weight of his recent failure pressed down upon him, a hulking burden that threatened to consume him entirely. He had acted with haste, with a zeal born of a misguided sense of celestial purpose. In his haste, he had taken a life, a far too young life. The guilt gnawed at him, a relentless predator that tore at his soul while his despair deepened.

He now saw himself as a flawed and sinful man. In a desperate attempt to atone for his transgression, he turned his self-loathing

## CHAPTER 5: FORGIVE ME FATHER, FOR I HAVE SINNED

inward. He reached for a leather belt, its worn surface a testament to countless nights of self-flagellation. With each strike, a sharp pain shot through his body, a physical manifestation of his spiritual anguish. Yet even this oddly extreme act of self-punishment was not enough. In a moment of madness, he reached for a razor, its cold, metallic edge glinting in the dim light. With trembling hands, he inflicted shallow cuts upon his flesh, each wound a testament to his remorse. The pain was intense, but it was nothing compared to the suffering that raged within him.

As the first rays of dawn pierced the darkness, the defanged Vindicator collapsed onto the floor, exhausted and broken. His body was marked with the scars of his self-inflicted suffering, a stark reminder of his self-envisioned fall from grace. But even as he lay there, his mind was still troubled. He knew that physical pain alone could not absolve him of his sins. He needed something more, something truly divine.

*Maybe Deacon Mancini, the preacher who condoned of strict penance could help?* He paused, no probably not, he needed a true priest- a pastor of the community who also had the Lord's power to forgive the sins of His flock. Maybe with a priest' official offering of reconciliation combined with his self-inflicted penance, his accidental mistake could truly be forgotten, and he can then overcome this emotional and spiritual setback. A flicker of hope ignited within him. *Perhaps*, he thought, *a priest could offer him the absolution he craved. A man of God, a conduit to the divine, could perhaps help him to find peace and redemption.* With renewed determination, he rose to his feet and made his way towards the nearest church.

The sun's golden beams pierced the morning sky, casting harsh light onto the streets below, where the usual hum of traffic and footfall filled the air. With the downturn in the number of attacks recently, more people bustled in and out of stores than normal, moving with the frenetic energy that came with a new day, unaware of the tormented soul that walked among them. The world, as it always did, continued in its relentless motion. But for the emotionally wounded figure formerly known as the Phantom, the brilliance of the sun felt almost cruel—an unforgiving reminder of the clarity he lacked, of the answers that still eluded him. It illuminated every corner of the city, and with it, the painful awareness of his own transgressions. Yet, despite the glaring light, despite the oppressive weight of his guilt, he felt an irresistible pull toward something familiar, something that had once offered him solace, the church.

The journey was not a conscious decision. His feet moved almost automatically, guided by a force greater than reason or logic. He had walked this path many times before, in both darkness and light, seeking refuge from the storm inside his mind. St. Patrick's Church had always been there for him, a sanctuary in a city where few things could be trusted. It was a place that provided quiet, an antidote to the chaos that swirled inside and outside of him. And now, as he found himself at its entrance, he was drawn toward it once more, seeking, though he knew not what, in the cool, sacred stillness of the church's interior.

The heavy wooden door creaked as he pushed it open, the sound reverberating in the stillness of the morning air. In an instant, the sharpness of the outside world seemed to fall away, as if the church were a world unto itself, apart from the relentless march of time. The contrast between the bright, unforgiving sunlight and the cool, dim interior of St. Patrick's was jarring. The moment he stepped inside, a wave of relief washed over him, though it was brief, as fleeting as the dim shadows that clung to the stone walls.

## CHAPTER 5: FORGIVE ME FATHER, FOR I HAVE SINNED

The air inside was cooler, the smell of old wood and incense permeating the space, calming the frenzy that had plagued him since the night before.

The silence was unmistakable, broken only by the faint echo of his footsteps on the marble floor. The high, vaulted ceilings loomed above him, casting the space in an almost otherworldly light as the sun filtered through the stained-glass windows. The colors from the glass danced across the stone floor, a kaleidoscope of reds, blues, and purples. To him, the sight was bittersweet. The windows were like fragmented pieces of a stained soul, beautiful yet broken, a reflection of his own fractured spirit. Here, in this sacred space, he was surrounded by symbols of faith, but none of them seemed to offer him the answers he sought. They were beautiful, yes, but distant, like a memory he couldn't quite grasp.

As he moved deeper into the church, his eyes fell upon the altar, the place of peace and sanctity. But even here, in the heart of the Lord's house, he still felt the weight of his sins. The very walls seemed to bear witness to his inner turmoil, and the flickering candles cast long shadows that whispered of things he could never undo. Despite the sense of peace that St. Patrick's offered, he was still a man filled with doubt, with guilt, and with the unshakeable feeling that he had crossed a line that could never be erased. His actions, though seemingly driven by a higher purpose, had left deep scars both on the people he had sought to save and on himself. He was no longer sure where the line between justice and vengeance had been drawn, and in this holy place, surrounded by relics of faith and mercy, he couldn't escape the heavy sense of responsibility that now anchored him. But the church was still a refuge, a place where he could confront the dark thoughts that lingered within him without the harsh judgment of the world outside. It was a place where he could strip away the mask of the Vindicator, the face of a vigilante, and for just a moment, be nothing more than a man—a man lost in his own regrets.

The chime of the large bell rang faintly from somewhere deep within the church as he made his way to the confessional, the worn wooden structure a testament to countless confessions whispered within its walls. Kneeling, he rested his forehead against the cold, hard wood, his breath misting the air. The soft murmur of prayers drifted through the church, a comforting hum in the background.

A low, gravelly voice interrupted his reverie. "And what brings you to the Lord's house today, my son?" The voice, thick with a Cajun-French accent, belonged to Father Landry, the well-known priest in the parish. He recognized the priest' familiar cadence, the same one that had offered him spiritual guidance on previous occasions so long ago.

As he began to confess his sins, the priest's keen senses detected the unmistakable scent of alcohol on his breath. A knowing smile creased the priest's lips as he interjected, "Ah, it seems the devil has tempted you with his fiery elixir early this fine morning." The lighthearted comment, delivered with a twinkle in his eye, momentarily eased the light tension that had gripped the confessor.

The troubled visitor grins and immediately begins to pour out his heart, confessing his sins one by one. But he does not say anything descriptive, that could incriminate himself in anything directly. He begins whimpering as he speaks of the pain and suffering, he has caused others through general statements. As he speaks, Father Landry listens intently, his heart filled with compassion. It's not out of the ordinary for a person to become emotional while confessing their sins to him, but it was what the visitor said next that was a revelation. He had asked for forgiveness for hurting people throughout his recent life, and that he feels immensely responsible and remorseful for his sins, and that he must have the Lord's forgiveness to go on with his life. Landry immediately remembered the words that many of the victims had reported hearing during the attacks: "I have been entrusted by our Father with immense responsibilities." He was triggered by those familiar words but kept his composure as he continued his duty to the intoxicated man. He gave him the usual prayer penance and asked him to do something nice for someone today.

Landry, the seasoned priest, was eerily stunned. A lingering doubt gnawed at his conscience. Could the man who had just unburdened his soul be the elusive Phantom, or Vindicator of Orleans? He had spent countless hours hearing confessions, but never had he imagined that the city's notorious attacker could possibly be sitting mere feet away. During the confession, the priest had leaned in, straining to see the man's face through the mesh screen meant to give the confessor a sense of anonymity. A familiar figure, yet strangely distorted, had emerged from the shade. He recognized the man from somewhere, a vague recollection flickering at the edge of his memory.

The Vindicator, a creature of myth and terror, had terrorized the city for months. His shadowy figure, cloaked in an aura of mystery, had haunted the streets, leaving a trail of fear and uncertainty. And now, this enigmatic figure could have sought solace in the very heart of the church, in search of absolution. Landry pondered the implications of this revelation. *Was it possible that the Vindicator, despite his dark deeds, harbored a conscience after all? Could this act of contrition be a sign of redemption, or merely a desperate ploy to evade justice?* The priest knew he had stumbled upon a mystery far more profound than any he had encountered in his long career.

He waited patiently, his eyes grazing between the small space in the confessional booth and the figure kneeling in front of him. He could sense that the man, though clearly distressed, was taking his time with his prayers of reconciliation. The low murmur of his whispered words mixed with the ambient sounds of the church—a few rustling pages, the faint echo of the organ playing somewhere in the distance. Despite the man's evident anguish, the priest gave him the space he needed. He knew from years of experience that confession was not merely about the words spoken; it was about allowing the penitent to wrestle with their own conscience in the presence of God.

A few minutes passed. Landry let his thoughts wander, reflecting on the man's earlier portion of the confession. There had been a rawness to his words, a deep sense of guilt that resonated through his every sentence. Many who came to him confessed feelings of being burdened by the weight of their actions or their duties. It was a common thread among his penitents. Still, the priest couldn't shake the nagging sensation that something was off, something about the visitor's presence seemed...familiar.

The sound of the man shifting on the pew broke Landry's reverie. The confession had concluded, and the visitor thanked Father Landry for his time. The man finally stood, and as he exited the dimly lit booth, a sense of relief washed over him. He could hear soft footfalls leaving the confessional booth as the figure rose to his feet and exited. Landry had trained himself to give his penitents the dignity of walking away from the confessional without feeling rushed or judged. He lingered for a few moments, waiting for the peculiar yet contrite man to walk away. The priest's gaze, though, was trained on the figure. The longer he watched through his entrance curtain, the more a sense of recognition began to grow in

## CHAPTER 5: FORGIVE ME FATHER, FOR I HAVE SINNED

the back of his mind.

He didn't immediately rise. His fingers lingered on the wooden edge of the confessional, the familiar texture offering him no comfort. He hesitated, listening to the soft sound of the man's footsteps fading into the ambient noise of the church. The churchgoer seemed to be walking slowly, purposefully, almost as though he were lost in thought, struggling with his own internal battle.

Landry waited a little longer, knowing that mass would soon begin. The church would be filled with the soft rustling of congregation members and the sound of the choir. It was only when the last prayerful silence filled the space that he decided to leave the confessional booth himself. Rising slowly, he tapped his hand against the old wood, taking a deep breath as he prepared to return to his daily duties. But something inside urged him to step into the main hall. As he did, he felt a subtle unease, a nagging pull. Landry glanced around for the man, and after a moment he sees him now on the move. His gaze followed the individual as he moved, seeing that the man had turned toward the back of the church, walking with a kind of heavy deliberation, as if deep in thought. His figure was dressed in plain, somber attire, nothing out of the ordinary, but something about his posture—the way he carried himself—was also oddly familiar. *Where had he seen him before?* Then it hit him, and his heart skipped a beat. The thought slammed into him with a cold shock. The voice, the words, the posture— he had spoken with this parishioner after mass before. The way he had confessed, the earnestness mixed with a strange tension in his movements, all fit the profile in his memory. Landry's stomach churned. *Could it really be him? Could this confessor really be the Vindicator, and if so, was it in fact the same man that he had met with previously, long before the reign of terror began?*

Landry's thoughts swirled, and he quickly realized that the man was making his way toward the exit. His brow furrowed, the weight of the situation becoming clearer with each passing moment. He felt torn, uncertain of what to do. He wasn't sure if the man truly could be the Vindicator, or simply someone who happened to share similar traits. The priest was no detective, his only weapon was faith accompanied with his sacred vow of silence. The confessions he heard within the walls of St. Patrick's Church were sacred, sealed by the eternal promise of secrecy. To ever reveal what he had just heard would be a betrayal, a break from the very principles that guided his life. Still, the man's aura—the mixture of guilt and righteousness, the sense that he was carrying the weight of something far greater than he could bear—was almost impossible to ignore. Landry moved toward the church's front entrance, hoping to catch another glimpse of the man as he exited. He stayed at a distance, careful not to draw unwanted attention to himself, as the figure approached the large wooden doors.

The man pushed them open, stepping into the sunlight, and Landry followed quietly, staying far enough back to avoid being seen. He watched as the man walked down the steps of the church, his movements now slower but deliberate. Landry's heart raced as he strained his eyes. There was no vehicle waiting outside, no car parked by the curb. The Vindicator had always been elusive—also never relying on vehicles, moving swiftly through the shadows. This figure's lack of transportation seemed to match his modus operandi.

The man continued down the block, blending into the active city street. Landry could no longer make out his features as he disappeared around the corner. It felt like a dream, like a surreal encounter that could be explained away by logic. But deep down,

## CHAPTER 5: FORGIVE ME FATHER, FOR I HAVE SINNED

Landry knew that he had witnessed something that could change everything. He stood motionless for a moment, his heart pounding in his chest. A sense of unease and urgency flooded through him. He had only known the notorious Vindicator by reputation, of course. The man who had taken justice into his own hands, who struck fear into the hearts of criminals and citizens alike. But now, standing in the aftermath of their encounter, Landry was unsure of what to do with this information. He had taken a vow of silence, one that bound him not only to the church but to the trust of those who came to him for absolution. *If this truly was the Vindicator,* Landry thought, *how could he prove it? What if he was mistaken? What if it was just a man struggling with his own demons, but not the one who had haunted the city's streets?* A cold sweat broke out on Landry's brow as he considered the alternative. *Should I break my vow? Should I tell the police?*

For the first time in a long while, the man of the cloth felt the weight of his position more acutely than ever. His role as a priest had always been clear-cut; offer solace, guidance, and absolution. But now, the murky waters of his moral responsibility seemed to pull him in a direction he wasn't sure he was ready to follow. How could he betray a trust he had sworn to uphold, even if the man in question was, indeed, the very one who had caused so much suffering and fear? Would it be his duty to stop him, or was he meant to remain a silent witness to the man's own redemption, if such a thing was even possible? Landry stood in the doorway of the church, his mind non-stop racing, torn between his duty as a man of God and his responsibility to the city, a city caught between fear and hope, between justice and vengeance.

# CHAPTER 6: A FAMILIAR FACE

Father Landry paced the small rectory, his mind racing with confusion and a growing sense of unease. He had been a priest in New Orleans for nearly two decades, long enough to recognize the faces and names of most of his parishioners. But the man who had confessed to him earlier that day was different, oddly familiar, yet elusive. As he replayed the details of the awkward confession in his mind, he couldn't shake the nagging feeling that something about the encounter was off. The man's voice, the way he spoke, even the words he used seemed strangely reminiscent of a familiar phrase—a phrase eerily similar to one that had been connected to the city's infamous attacker.

The more Landry thought about it, the more the pieces began to fit together, like fragments of a puzzle he hadn't realized he was putting together. The confession itself had been unsettling, but it was the manner in which the man had spoken—his tone, his hesitancy—that lingered in his thoughts. The memories seemed to fall into place slowly, and then, while sipping on his morning cup of coffee, it finally came to him in a rush of clarity. Yes, he had definitely seen this man before. It wasn't just a fleeting encounter; this was someone who had visited the church multiple times in the past. He wasn't a regular parishioner, but rather someone who would appear intermittently after mass, speaking of his struggles, his guilt, and his desperate desire for redemption.

The priest remembered the way the man had always seemed grateful for his counsel, often expressing his thanks with a generous donation at the end of their conversations. The envelopes he would leave behind, neatly filled with money, were always presented with a certain sense of urgency, as if the man were desperate to atone for something, to make up for the weight of whatever burden he was carrying. But now, with the confession still echoing in his mind, Landry couldn't help but wonder if there was more to this man's story than he had let on. Was he really seeking redemption, or was something far darker at play?

The more he thought about it, the more he felt he was right about the visitor. Everything was making sense. The man who had confessed to him earlier was fixated on religious redemption, his guilt, his belief that he had been "entrusted with immense responsibilities"—it all fit too well. The confessor's words, his fervent desire for atonement, his obsession with sin, rang loud in Landry's mind. *This man—could he really be the Vindicator of Orleans?* He had to be right. This man had to be the notorious figure who had haunted the city for months, his crimes shrouded in mystery, his true motives unknown. Landry's heart pounded as the connection formed in his mind. *But how could he be sure? How could he prove it?*

Landry knew that suspicion alone wasn't enough. He needed more. Something tangible, something concrete that would confirm his suspicions. The confessor had been a semi-frequent visitor to the church, often seen praying alone in the back pews, his face hidden in shadow as he sat for hours in deep contemplation. He had even volunteered once to help with one of the church's community activities, his quiet demeanor and willingness to serve making him seem like any other devout parishioner. But now, in the wake of the confession, those same behaviors seemed less innocent. *Could it be that this man—this possible suspect—had used his familiarity with the church to carefully plan his attacks? Was his devotion merely a cover for something darker, a tool he wielded to further his twisted sense of righteousness?*

His mind raced as he considered the implications. *Had this man chosen his victims not by random chance, but based solely on their perceived sins? Could he truly believe that he was carrying out God's will, doling out divine punishment for those he deemed unworthy, all to avoid Gehenna?* The more Landry thought about it, the more chilling the possibility seemed. The Vindicator had always been a figure of mystery, his actions both violent and methodical, but if he was truly driven by religious zealotry that twisted the very notion of justice, it would explain so much. It would mean that the man sitting in the confessional, seeking absolution for his own sins, might very well be the one responsible for the carnage that had terrorized the city. The more the anxious priest thought about it, the more convinced he became that he was, in fact, in the company of the city's tormentor. Every detail from the confession—the man's obsessive need for redemption, his sense of responsibility, his cryptic references to divine judgment—lined up too perfectly with the behavior of the city's phantom assailant. The eerie familiarity, the strange blend of piety and guilt, it all pointed to one conclusion. The man sitting in his confessional had to be the infamous attacker

## CHAPTER 6: A FAMILIAR FACE

who had eluded the police for all this time, terrorizing the area with his brutal crimes. But despite his growing certainty, Landry knew that proving it wouldn't be easy. Especially without knowing the man's name. If it was him, he was a cunning and dangerous individual, a master of evasion, and he would do everything in his power to avoid being caught.

His thoughts swirled with conflicting emotions. On the one hand, he knew he couldn't keep this information to himself. If the man truly was the Phantom/Vindicator, then every day that passed without action put more innocent lives at risk. On the other hand, sharing his suspicions with anyone, especially law enforcement, was a dangerous proposition. The Vindicator's reach seemed to extend far beyond his crimes; his control over the city, the church, and even those who should have been his allies were unsettling. Father Landry had seen firsthand how the attacker's presence had infiltrated the lives of the people around him. He couldn't afford to make a mistake, and he couldn't take the risk of acting rashly.

Finally, after hours of internal deliberation, Landry made up his mind. He knew that if he was going to stop this man, he couldn't do it alone. It was time to share his suspicions with the detectives investigating the case: Baptiste and Foret. His two new friends had been relentless in their pursuit of the Vindicator, their commitment to bringing him to justice unwavering. Landry knew they had the resources and expertise to build a stronger case, to find the evidence that would finally connect this man to the crimes. They would be able to investigate his past, his movements, his connections, and perhaps uncover the missing pieces of the perplexing puzzle. But as the thought of reaching out to the detectives settled in his mind, a wave of fear washed over Landry. He wasn't just exposing the potential identity of a killer; he was putting himself in direct danger. This was not just a faceless criminal; he was possibly the man driven by delusion and a warped sense of extreme justice. If he was correct, if the man sitting in his confessional really was who he thought he was, then revealing that knowledge could make him a target. What if the attacker knew Landry had suspected him? What if his confession had been part of some twisted game, an attempt to lure the priest into his web? His pulse quickened at the thought. He was acutely aware of the risks involved in crossing this fanatic. The man was ruthless and had proven time and time again that he had no hesitation in accomplishing his goals. The idea of sharing his suspicions with Baptiste and Foret was not a decision he made lightly. It meant that his life, along with the lives of those closest to him, could be at risk. But the more he thought about it, the more he understood that there was no other choice. He had been entrusted with the confessions of the guilty, and now he held a piece of information that could potentially save lives. His moral responsibility was clear: he couldn't just sit idle, even if it meant breaking his vow or putting himself directly in harm's way.

That evening, after the last mass had ended and the church had emptied, Landry sat in the quiet of the rectory, drafting his thoughts carefully. He knew how much he was risking by stepping forward, but the truth had to come out. He picked up the phone and dialed Detective Baptiste's number, his hand trembling slightly as the line rang. There was no turning back now, the finality of his decision settled over him like a heavy cloak. He wouldn't be able to stay in the rectory any longer, pacing and second-guessing his decision. He knew what he had to do, the moment of truth had arrived.

Leaving the safety of his home felt like stepping into the unknown, a dangerous journey that could change everything. He

## CHAPTER 6: A FAMILIAR FACE

slipped on his worn, brown overcoat and stepped into the muggy, damp New Orleans evening air; his breath visible in the foggy streetlights. The city felt different tonight—darker, more oppressive—as if it, too, sensed the weight of what was about to unfold. He had walked these streets for years, had seen them in every season, in every mood. He knew the alleys and the quiet corners, the creaking iron balconies, the hum of distant music in the night. But tonight, something about the familiar landscape felt alien to him. There was tension in the air, creeping dread that settled in his chest as he began walking towards the police station. His steps echoed in the narrow streets, the sound amplifying in the stillness around him. And in that stillness, he couldn't shake the feeling that he was being watched.

It was absurd, of course, he was a priest, a servant of God. *Why would anyone be paying attention to him?* And yet, the hairs on the back of his neck stood on end, his senses heightened in a way he couldn't explain. Perhaps it was the gravity of the situation pressing down on him, or the overwhelming knowledge that by revealing his suspicions, he was stepping into a world far more dangerous than the sanctity of his arena, the church. He had no illusions now. This wasn't just about bringing justice to a handful of victims, it was about confronting a force that had transformed the city, that had made his sacred duties feel small and helpless in comparison to the gloom it wrought.

The thought of the countless victims filled him with a renewed sense of resolve. Each of the past attacks had left a mark on the city—one of fear, confusion, and sorrow. The people of New Orleans were his flock, and like any shepherd, he had a responsibility to protect them, to guide them through the dark times. He had heard their confessions, listened to their pleas for forgiveness, and helped them navigate their life's struggles. And now, the very same faith he had instilled in others was calling on him to do the same, to walk the difficult and dangerous road to justice. No matter what the cost.

With each step, the weight of his mission settled heavier on his shoulders. His legs moved mechanically, almost as if his body were acting on its own, driven by something deeper than fear. He knew he was doing the right thing, there was no question about that. But the truth was, he had no idea what was waiting for him at the end of this journey. What would happen when he walked into that police station? Would Baptiste and Foret agree with him? Or would they dismiss him, as a man desperate for a connection that didn't exist?

The Vindicator was clever, too shrewd to be caught easily. Landry had seen the way the city's detectives had struggled to piece together the clues, the way he had always been one step ahead. What if the man in the confessional knew about the investigation? What if he had been watching Landry this entire time, planting the seed of suspicion in his mind? Could the Vindicator have orchestrated this entire encounter, manipulating the priest into bringing his crumbs to the police, thus exposing himself as an informant, and revealing the exact detectives that were on his trail?

# CHAPTER 7: SPEAK NO EVIL

Following the officer from behind the front desk, Father Landry could hear the clatter of ringing phones and the hum of footsteps fading into the background as he made his way down the sterile hallways toward the office of his favorite Detectives, Baptiste and Foret. He had been there a few times before, throughout the lengthy investigation. But this time he felt different, his every step felt weighted with more purpose than before. The knot of anxiety in his stomach only tightened as he approached their door. It wasn't normal practice for a priest to engage in conversations about someone's private confession, but these were not ordinary circumstances.

The detectives greeted him warmly, their smiles a stark contrast to the anxiety that had settled deep in his chest.

"Father, good to see you!" Foret said, his voice was a mix of joviality and concern. The older detective leaned back in his chair, his eyes scanning Landry as if trying to read the unspoken tension in his face.

"You look like you've seen a ghost."

"I wish it were just that," Landry replied, forcing a smile that didn't quite reach his eyes. He felt the weight of his clerical collar pressing down on him like an iron shackle, a reminder of the vow he had taken to protect the sanctity of holy confession. Yet, in this instance, he sensed a divine urgency, a compulsion to speak up for God's people that he could not ignore. His mind once again replayed the confession, its unsettling tone, the ominous words—and he couldn't shake the feeling that he was on the cusp of relaying a stunning piece of information, one that might alter the course of several lives. He had wrestled with what to do all night, but now he felt compelled to move forward.

As he took a seat across from the detectives, he glanced out the window behind their desks, half-expecting to see a hooded figure lurking in the alleys below. His walk to the station had been filled with a creeping sense of paranoia, an unsettling feeling that he was being watched. The city had always felt alive in a way that teetered on the edge of chaos, but now, the weight of the media's obsession with the phantom attacker—the "Vindicator"—made it feel even more dangerous. And as Landry's thoughts drifted back to the man he had spoken with in confession, *could he be the one responsible for the violence that had been sweeping through the streets for weeks and weeks?*

Baptiste, a woman with sharp eyes and a calm demeanor, watched him carefully. She had been through enough cases to recognize when something was off, and right now, she could tell that Landry was carrying a heavy burden.

"Father, what's on your mind?" Baptiste prodded gently, her voice low and understanding. She could sense the hesitation in his posture, the tension in his hands as they gripped the armrests.

Landry exhaled deeply, drawing on his faith for strength. With a

## CHAPTER 7: SPEAK NO EVIL

measured voice, he began to recount the details of the confession.

"A man came to me for confession earlier," he began. "He was troubled, speaking of vengeance and righteousness as if they were one and the same. He believed he was to be punished for his acts, and he spoke in riddles." He paused, his throat tight. "The weight of his words were like nothing I'd ever felt before. It was an intense darkness in the confessional—a kind of malevolence I couldn't ignore."

Foret's brow furrowed, his tone shifting to one of seriousness. "Do you feel like this is connected to the Vindicator?"

Landry's eyes darkened. "I can't say for certain. But it sure felt like a revelation. I've never experienced anything like it. He even mentioned being 'immensely responsible' for his sins."

Landry's hands gripped the edges of the chair, as if to steady himself. "The words weren't exact, but they were close enough to make me think there's a connection."

The detectives exchanged glances, their expressions shifting from curiosity to urgency. Baptiste, ever the level-headed one, leaned forward, her eyes narrowing even more as she absorbed the weight of Landry's words.

"Did he mention any specific names or events?" she asked, her voice clipped.

Landry shook his head. "No, not exactly. He spoke vaguely, but 'there was something' in his eyes—a fire, a fervor—that I could see even through the confessional screen. It chilled me. Even though he was there for confession, I could feel that he believed he was intimately linked to the Lord, almost like answering to a boss of some sort. Like he was trying to do God's will."

The detectives fell silent, the weight of what Landry was saying settling heavily in the room. Baptiste's fingers drummed lightly on the desk as she processed the information.

"This is huge," Foret murmured. "You might have just given us the break we've been looking for. If there's even the smallest chance this guy's involved... we can't ignore it."

Baptiste's expression hardened. "We need to follow up on this lead immediately. If there's even a chance he's connected to the Vindicator, we must act. The stakes are too high."

Landry nodded slowly, though unease gnawed at him. His gut twisted, a deep sense of foreboding settling into his bones. He couldn't shake the feeling that he had just placed himself in the crosshairs.

"I fear I may have just put a target on my back," he murmured, his voice barely above a whisper.

Baptiste met his gaze, her expression softening. "Father, you did what was right. You've given us something crucial, something we wouldn't have had without your insight. We'll make sure you're safe. This is bigger than any one of us."

Landry looked up at her, the enormity of what he had just revealed sinking in. It wasn't just about the killer anymore—it was about his role in this mess, about his very life being entangled in the search for justice. The city was at war with itself, and now, he was part of the battle.

As the detectives scribbled notes, Landry's mind wandered back to the faith that had always steadied him in moments of doubt. He had always believed that he was an instrument of God's will, but in this moment, he couldn't shake the feeling that he was being led into a storm without any kind of divine protection. He had prayed for clarity, for guidance—but the path ahead felt like one of peril. He had no way of knowing where it would lead.

"Can you describe the man at all?" Foret asked, breaking the

## CHAPTER 7: SPEAK NO EVIL

silence. "Any distinguishing features?"

Landry nodded, his mind drifting back to the face of the man in the confessional.

"He was kind of tall, disheveled, with a light beard that looked unkempt. He smelled of alcohol, and his eyes..." He paused, his voice faltering for a moment. "His eyes were the worst part. There was a kind of madness in them. A fervor that made my skin crawl. I've seen him before, but he definitely looked different than the few times I'd seen him before."

Foret's pen scratched rapidly across the notepad. His eyes widened as he processed the details.

"So, you'd seen him before, but you don't remember his name, right?"

Landry nodded affirmatively, and Foret continues. "Well, this matches the profile given by several witnesses from the scenes of the attacks. We need to get this information out to our teams immediately."

Baptiste nodded sharply, her tone now resolute. "We'll get the word out. If this man is the one we're looking for, we can't afford to waste any time."

Landry sat back in his chair, the weight of the situation pressing down on him like an anvil. He had done what he could, and the rest was now in their hands. And as the detectives began organizing their next steps, Landry couldn't shake the thought that he had just opened a door to something far darker than he had ever imagined. The Vindicator was no longer just a story in the papers. He was very real. And now, Father Landry was even more part of the chase.

Just as the anxious Landry opened his mouth to continue, a sudden commotion outside of the office broke his concentration. The sharp clatter of boots echoed down the hallway, and voices raised in urgency cut through the air. He could hear a door slam open, followed by the distinctive rhythm of officers moving in a frantic hurry. Then, a shout rang out from the hallway, loud enough to shake the quiet intensity of the room.

"We've got a good lead! We think we've found him! He was just spotted near St. Patrick's Church on Camp Street! Let's go, move it, move it!"

Baptiste and Foret sprang to their feet in perfect unison, their bodies instantly on high alert, to join in the stampede. Landry froze, his heart suddenly in his throat as a new chill ran through him. The adrenaline in the air was intense, and for a moment, the room felt too small. Landry's pulse quickened, his thoughts colliding with his instincts. He had just shared his suspicion, his revelation, but this... this was spontaneous and real. They were possibly on the verge of something monumental—and of course, dangerous.

"Wait!" Landry called out; his voice was louder than he intended. He stood abruptly, the chair scraping harshly against the floor.

"This man I spoke of—he's probably dangerous! If he thinks he's on a mission from God, there's no telling what he might do!" The words tumbled out in a rush, fear creeping into his voice. He hadn't fully processed the full scope of what he was saying until the words were already spilling out of him. This was no ordinary suspect. The man was driven by an unshakable belief in his divine mission, and the consequences of that belief could, and would be catastrophic.

Baptiste and Foret paused for a split second, their expressions hardening. They exchanged a brief, knowing look, and Landry could see the unspoken calculation pass between them. This was no longer just a matter of tracking down a criminal—it was about managing the unpredictability of someone who believed they were acting in the name of God. Landry's warning hung in the air, heavy and ominous.

"We'll handle it from here, Father, this is what we do best," Baptiste said, her voice calm but firm.

There was no question in her tone, no room for debate. She turned toward the door, her hand already on the handle.

"You've done your part today. Lay low, and just stay here for your own safety. We'll be in touch, hopefully after we've picked up your guy."

Foret nodded in agreement, his brow also furrowed in concentration as he grabbed his jacket.

"You did what you could, Father. We got it from here."

Landry's chest tightened, a cold knot formed in the pit of his stomach. He opened his mouth to protest, to offer more, but the words got caught in his throat. It wasn't that he didn't trust Baptiste and Foret—they had proven themselves capable and determined in the face of danger, but this was different. This man, whoever he was, had confessed his sins while simultaneously justifying the violence he had already committed, and perhaps more he intended to commit. He had entrusted his darkest secrets to him, instantly linking them permanently. There was no telling what kind of madness lay beneath that man's facade.

The thought of the Vindicator being near the old church on Camp Street unsettled him. That church—his church—was a place of refuge for the lost and broken. It wasn't just a building; it was a part of his soul. And if this man was truly out there, believing his violent acts were somehow divine, Landry couldn't ignore the feeling that he still may be in the vicinity of the church expecting to find sanctuary...or worse yet, looking for him.

But the detectives were already in motion. Baptiste moved with purposeful speed, followed by Foret, both of them well-trained to act on a moment's notice. Landry stood there, immobilized by the weight of his own thoughts. A swirl of conflicting emotions rose within him. Fear for the people of the city, for the victims yet to be claimed by the Vindicator; guilt, for the secrets he carried in the silence of the confessional, and a gnawing sense of helplessness. He had spoken the truth, but was it enough? Was it too little, too late?

As the door clicked shut behind the detectives, Landry found himself alone in the musky room. He could still hear the hurried steps of the officers in the hallway, their frantic pace reverberating through the walls. He glanced out the window once more, scanning the darkening streets below, half-expecting to see the man from his confession—tall, disheveled, eyes full of madness—lurking in the distant shadows. His fingers twitched involuntarily. A prayer slipped from his lips, though he wasn't sure whom he was praying for. Was it God, to spare the city from more bloodshed? Or was it for himself, to give him the strength to see this through? He stood by the window for a long moment, his heart racing, his mind torn between the call of his faith and the brutal reality unfolding outside. He had done what he could. He had warned the detectives, offered his insights, and now all he could do was wait. Wait, and pray.

He sat down in the chair they had vacated, hands clasped tightly together in his lap. His mind raced, but his body remained still, seeking solace in the eventual silence. He closed his eyes, whispering another prayer, this time with more urgency.

"Lord, protect me, protect the innocent and guide my steps in these perilous times."

His voice faltered slightly, as if the words were a shield, something to protect him from the gnawing uncertainty settling into his bones.

Outside, the unmistakable sound of sirens wailed, growing louder as they echoed through the narrow streets, reverberating off the stone buildings of the city. A siren's song, always crying for help, always a sign of danger. The city was on the brink, trembling on the edge of something tragic. Landry couldn't shake the thought that, by walking into this office, by sharing his suspicions, he had unknowingly lit a fuse. A fuse that was about to ignite an even greater conflagration, one that could consume more lives than he could bear to imagine.

The knot in his stomach tightened. The weight of his faith, of his vows, pressed down on him like an anchor, trying to keep him grounded in the swirling chaos. But even in his turmoil, Landry knew that there was no turning back now. Whatever new tribulations lay ahead, he would face them bravely. His trust in God was the only thing keeping him from falling into despair. He had already taken the first step, and he couldn't undo it now. He had spoken, had made himself a part of this battle between good and evil, and in this war, there were no simple victories. There were only choices—choices that could save lives or condemn them. He could already feel and hear the low rumble of the hell storm approaching.

The thought of staying in the station, waiting for news, felt suffocating. The unease from the walk to the police headquarters, the nagging sense that he was being watched, returned with vengeance. He stood up abruptly, his decision made. He couldn't remain there. He needed to get back home—back to the church, to the refuge he had always known. There, he could pray, regroup, and find the additional strength to continue.

Landry reached for his light jacket and made his way to the door. Once he exited the antique building, something in the back of his mind clicked. A feeling, instinctual and primal, swept over him—the unmistakable sensation of eyes once again on his back. The hair on the back of his neck stood on end, and he froze mid-step, his pulse hammering in his ears. *Had he truly been followed?* He turned sharply, scanning the street behind him, but it was empty, quiet. No one else was there. Yet, the eerie feeling persisted, sharp and unnerving.

As he continued up the street, the cool evening air hit his face, sharp and biting. His eyes scanned the street, looking for anything out of place. The city felt desolate, the streets somber, the darkness deeper. He quickened his pace, instincts now fully alert, his every step shadowed by an unshakable feeling that someone was trailing him. The feeling intensified as Landry moved down the street, the familiar sights of the city were suddenly unfamiliar. The streets of the city that care forgot, once full of life and music, felt eerily empty. He could hear his own footsteps echoing back at him, as if the city itself was holding its breath. He pushed the nervous thoughts aside, focusing on putting more distance between himself and the station. Just get home. Get safe. Unbeknownst to Landry, there was a person carefully trailing him and he wasn't just any stranger, but the very man he had spoken of in the confessional—the one he had warned Baptiste about. The Vindicator was closer than he realized, just out of view, stalking the priest he had recently confided in.

Landry's heart hammered in his chest as he pushed open the heavy wooden door that led into his modest quarters, the small residence tucked behind the church. The comforting scent of incense and old wood filled his nostrils, but tonight it didn't do much to calm his frayed nerves. He had barely made it inside when the

## CHAPTER 7: SPEAK NO EVIL

feeling of being followed, the sensation that someone—had been watching him, surged back. He quickly shut and bolted the door behind him, the old lock clicking with a finality that did little to ease the tension in his shoulders. The church and rectory's stone walls, once a sanctuary from the world's chaos, now felt more like a cage. The thick silence around him only seemed to amplify his unease, the stillness of the place somehow denser than usual, as if the weight of his own actions had become tangible.

He stood for a moment in the foyer, his hand still on the door. The familiar flicker of candlelight from the small chapel beyond the hall caught his eye, but he didn't move toward it. He couldn't. This long day, the confession, the encounter with the detectives, and the overwhelming sensation of being watched drained him. Every instinct told him to take shelter, to close himself off from the rest of the world. *The Vindicator. The man was out there. And perhaps, just perhaps, he was already here.* He closed his eyes for a moment, wishing the tension to leave his body. He took a slow, steadying breath, and when he opened his eyes again, he forced himself to move forward, into the chapel. The old wooden pews were empty, as they always were at this hour. He made his way to the altar, kneeling slowly, feeling the cool stone beneath him. There, he bowed his head and prayed—prayed for the safety of his people, for the souls of the city, for the strength to face whatever came next. His words flowed from him, but there was an edge to them, a desperation that hadn't been there before.

"Lord, give me guidance", he whispered into silence. "I ask you again, please give me the strength to see this through to the very end, no matter the cost."

But even as he briefly prayed, the concerning fear returned, intensifying in his chest again. He unexplainably could still feel the eyes on him—*not just from God, but from something darker*—and that awareness sharpened as the minutes stretched on. The darkness outside had only deepened with the night, and the sounds of officers and sirens that were recently covering his block had dispersed with no capture of the fugitive. Their sounds faintly fading away through the thick, ancient stone. He stepped further into his home, his breath coming in uneven bursts. The door closed behind him with a soft thud, and he felt a strange sense of finality, as though crossing the threshold had sealed him into a world of uncertainty and danger. He was finally beginning to calm some as he accepted the fact that the authorities did not find anyone of interest around his domicile.

He finally moved into the small living area, a simple space with a worn couch, a few chairs, and a small wooden table in the center. The faint light from the chapel cast long shadows against the walls, and the ticking of the old grandfather clock in the corner was the only sound in the room, a constant reminder of the time slipping away, unnoticed. Landry's eyes drifted toward the small crucifix hanging on the wall above the table, the figure of Christ looking down at him with an expression of quiet compassion. He had long found absolute solace in this space, in these walls that had witnessed so many of his prayers, his moments of peace, his own confessions. But tonight, these same walls felt as though they were closing in on him, pressing in with their silent judgment. He glanced out of the small window that looked out onto the grounds of the church. The night was still, save for the occasional rustling of leaves in the wind. The bell tower loomed over the landscape, silent for now, but it felt as though it was watching him too—an ancient sentinel, never blinking.

A noise from behind made him turn sharply, but there was

nothing—just the creaking of the old floorboards beneath his feet, the sound of a house settling, nothing more. Still, his pulse continued to slightly race. The thought was chilling, and it gripped him in an iron fist. He was part of something much larger now, something that he could not escape, no matter how hard he tried. The man who had come to him for confession—the man who he felt had to be the Vindicator—was still out there. And tonight, it still seemed that he had come home with Landry. His hands trembled slightly as he clasped them in prayer once again, his voice rising with a renewed urgency. But now, the walls that had once protected him were becoming a cage. He was no longer just the shepherd of his flock—he was part of the flock, and the wolf was closing in.

# CHAPTER 8: BLASPHEMOUS TONGUE

Father Landry awoke to the soft, melodic chirps of birds in the early morning, their songs carrying through the cool, fresh air of dawn. The first rays of sunlight filtered through the stained-glass windows of his quaint rectory, casting colorful patterns across the room. For a moment, the peaceful scene might have seemed serene, a quiet start to another day. Yet, the tranquility of the morning did little to ease the restlessness that had plagued him for the past several hours. His sleep had been fitful, interrupted by nightmares and anxious thoughts. The growing fear of the city's infamous tormentor weighed heavily on his mind, chewing at his thoughts like an unrelenting force. He could not shake the anxiety that had crept into his daily life, a constant worry that the Vindicator might find him next. Though unlikely, it was still a terrifying thought. Was it truly a crazy idea to fear that the notorious figure would seek him out in the very place that should offer spiritual refuge—the church?

## CHAPTER 8: BLASPHEMOUS TONGUE

The parish rectory, a small, humble building tucked away behind the grand edifice of the church, had always been a place of peaceful solitude for Landry. It was quiet, simple, and close enough to the heart of the archdiocese to allow him to fulfill his duties with ease. Yet, in the face of the Vindicator's wrath, the security of this little building seemed almost laughable. The idea that someone so dangerous might make their way into this very shelter was enough to make his skin crawl. Until recently, the lack of security had never seemed like an issue. The rectory's solitude had been a blessing, a serene retreat where he could reflect on his work and his faith. But now, after his recent visit to the police station, he found himself looking over his shoulder frequently, unsure whether his place of solace had now become his greatest vulnerability.

After a quick breakfast—more out of routine than hunger—Landry made his way to the church to begin his morning duties. His three-hour shift hearing confessions was a sacred part of his role as a priest, a time when he could offer guidance, absolution, and comfort to troubled parishioners. But today, the weight of his duties pressed heavily on him.

As the morning wore on and the sun climbed higher in the sky, he heard the curtain slide open and someone enter before closing the dark maroon curtain again. In seconds a familiar scent began to seep through the confessional screen. It was a smell that made his stomach quickly churn: the unmistakable combination of stale body odor and cheap alcohol. It was a scent he had recently encountered before, but this time, it brought with it a rush of panic. His heart began to speed up, and a cold sweat broke out across his brow again, as his mind made the connection. He had smelled this same odor in a previous confession—the one that had been lodged in his memory ever since. This was no ordinary parishioner. This was the person he feared most in the city—the very one who might be the infamous Vindicator.

Landry's pulse quickened, and his hands trembled slightly as he adjusted his position, trying to steady his nerves. The confessional, which had always been a place of solace, now felt suffocating, the air thick with the tension of the moment. He forced himself to breathe deeply, trying to push aside the growing sense of dread that was threatening to overtake him. The man on the other side of the screen spoke first, his voice gravelly and low.

"Good morning, Father."

The greeting was almost casual, but Landry could hear the underlying edge to it, as if the man knew something Landry was too afraid to acknowledge.

He hesitated for a moment, swallowing hard as his nerves threatened to betray him. He stuttered slightly as he responded, his voice tight with uncertainty.

"G-G-Good day, Son."

He was doing his best to sound calm, to maintain his composure, but inside he was spiraling. The man's presence, the smell of him, the weight of his words—it all felt like an impending storm that was closing in around him. He had no way of knowing for sure whether this man was the Vindicator, but the fear in his heart told him that it was far too much of a coincidence. *Why would he be back so soon?*

The disheveled man continued, his words deliberate, almost ritualistic:

"In the name of the Father, the Son, and the Holy Spirit. Forgive me, Father, for I have sinned."

The cadence of the words, the way they hung in the air, felt wrong somehow. Landry's ears rang, and he found it difficult to

## CHAPTER 8: BLASPHEMOUS TONGUE

focus on the man's assertion. His heart throbbed in his chest, drowning out everything around him. He could hardly hear the man's words over the thundering of his own heartbeat. It was all he could do to keep his mind from spinning out of control. Every instinct screamed at him to run, to call for help, to do anything but stay there cornered in the confessional with a man who might very well be the Vindicator. But he remained, frozen in place, unsure of what would happen next, and terrified of what it might mean for him—and for the city—if he were to be right.

Suddenly, like a vicious striking cobra, the hooded figure lunged forward, punching through the small screen separating them. The force of the unsuspecting blow sent Landry reeling backward. The loud noise startled the rest of the church, and a light panic erupted among the few parishioners present, their prayers cut short by the sudden commotion. As the hooded figure hastily ripped open his side of the confessional curtain, he emerged from the wooden booth, closing in on Landry's position. The startled priest continued to stumble out of the adjacent curtain, trying to get to his feet, his mind racing with shock. Most of the bystanders begin fleeing from the church, but a few stay, looking on in horror, as the hooded man, lunges again at the off-balance cleric. Like he had done so many times in the past, he grabs Landry by his neck, and throws him down, pinning him on the marble floor. The attacker's eyes, cold and devoid of any mercy, seemed to bore into Landry's soul. With a chilling calm, he raised his knife, its blade shimmering in the dense light.

"You will no longer speak out against me or our Father ever again!" he hissed, his voice a chilling whisper.

As the knife descended, Landry's uneven screams echoed through the church, a haunting cry that would forever be etched in the memories of those who heard it. The church had turned into a scene of total chaos, as the attacker quickly ran for the exit.

Parishioners, their faces pale with shock and horror, scrambled toward the injured priest, their movements clumsy and frantic. Some of them instinctively knelt beside him, trying to assess his injuries, while others stood frozen, staring in disbelief at the hectic scene unfolding before them. The tranquil sanctuary, once filled with the soft murmur of prayer, was now overwhelmed by the frantic cries of confusion and fear. The priest, his hand pressed to his face in an attempt to staunch the blood, winced as his parishioners surrounded him, their faces a mix of concern and terror.

Amidst the chaos, one thought persisted in the minds of the witnesses: *Could this attacker be the vaunted Vindicator?* But why would such a figure choose to strike at a priest, a man of the cloth who had spent his life in service to others? Wasn't the priest one of the few in this broken world who could be counted on to sin the least? Surely, there were far worse people in the city—those whose deeds were far more deserving of such brutal judgment. The questions swirled in the minds of the onlookers, unanswered and full of dread.

The attack itself had been quick and brutal as usual, the kind of violence that left no room for explanation, no chance for mercy. The Vindicator was known for his cold efficiency, and this sure seemed like his work. He never lingered, never gave his victims—whether guilty or innocent—time to plead or beg. As quickly as the attack had begun, the figure had disappeared into the thick morning mist that clung to the streets like a shroud. It was as though he had never been there at all, his presence now only a haunting memory in the air. As was his way, he had vanished into the streets, leaving behind nothing but the trail of terror in his

## CHAPTER 8: BLASPHEMOUS TONGUE

wake. The parishioners could do little more than watch helplessly as the morning light filtered through the stained-glass windows, casting long, eerie shadows across the bloody scene. The priest, now gasping for breath, gargled on his blood, the faint whisper of his moans as the scene around him continued in a frenzy of horror. His fate now hung in the balance, his life seemingly slipping away as uncertainty gripped the hearts of all who witnessed the attack. *If him, would the Vindicator return to strike again? And if so, who would be next?* After this type of brash assault, no one was safe, not even the spiritual men who had devoted their lives to healing souls.

The horrifically wounded priest lay on the cold, damp floor, his upper body a bloody mess. The pain was excruciating, but his mind raced with thoughts of his attacker's escape, and the danger he posed to others in the city. One thing was certain, he was right from the beginning. He had been in the company of the Vindicator, literally inches away from him! If this crazed lunatic was this brazen to pull off an unspeakable event like this in broad daylight, at a church of all places, he would be truly capable of doing just about anything at this point. He knew he still had to find a way to help his friends stop this madman, no matter what the cost. He would not let the Vindicator's reign of terror continue. He would rally the people and the authorities with what he went through today, because the city's tormentor must be brought to justice.

As the panic in the church swirled and the air thickened with fear, the wail of the sirens grew louder, cutting through the chaos. The distant sound of approaching paramedics finally pierced the thick fog of uncertainty that had settled over the room. Minutes seemed to stretch like hours, but at last, the ambulances screeched to a halt outside the church, their flashing lights reflecting off the stained-glass windows, creating an eerie kaleidoscope of colors within.

Two paramedics rushed through the church doors, their boots pounding against the stone floor, their faces set in grim determination. They quickly assessed the scene: the body of Father Landry sprawled on the floor, bloodstaining the front of his cassock, and the faces of the terrified parishioners looking on, helpless and panicked. One paramedic, a woman with short, dark hair and steady hands, dropped to her knees beside her new patient. She immediately placed her fingers on his neck, checking for a pulse. A small sigh of relief escaped her lips when she felt it, weak but steady.

"He's still with us, but he's lost a lot of blood," she said quickly, her voice cutting through the murmurs of the onlookers. "We need to move him quickly. Get him on a stretcher, now!"

Another paramedic, a tall man with a grim expression, moved swiftly to the priest's side, his hands working efficiently as he and his partner gently lifted Father Landry onto the stretcher. His blood continued to seep through a man's shirt being used as a makeshift tourniquet, and his breathing was shallow, his face pale and slick with sweat. The paramedics worked quickly, but there was no mistaking the gravity of the situation. He was badly injured and blood flowing from his face, a sight that left even the hardened first responders grimacing.

The crowd parted like the Red Sea as the paramedics began to wheel the stretcher toward the exit. People backed away, some of them crossing themselves, others whispering prayers under their breath, trying to make sense of what had just happened. The atmosphere was heavy with a sense of helplessness, and a collective understanding that something far larger than just one random attack was now unfolding in their midst. Outside, the paramedics lifted Landry into the back of the ambulance with practiced speed,

## CHAPTER 8: BLASPHEMOUS TONGUE

slamming the doors shut behind them. One of the paramedics shouted to the driver, "Let's roll!"

The ambulance sped off, its sirens blaring through the empty streets, cutting through the stillness that had descended on the city. In the back of the vehicle, Father Landry's eyes fluttered, a faint groan escaping his lips as he slowly regained a semblance of consciousness. He tried to speak, but his voice was unrecognizable, barely a whisper. Nothing but a low slurring murmur. The female paramedic leaned closer to him, her face softening with sympathy, but she couldn't respond to what she thought was a question. There were no answers, not yet. There was only the immediate task of saving his life.

"We're on our way to University Medical Center, Father," she said, her tone gentle but firm. "Stay with us. Stay awake."

Back inside the church, the remaining parishioners gathered in small clusters, some still in shock, others comforting one another with whispered prayers. The attack on Father Landry was not just an assault on a man of faith—it was a blow to the very heart of the community. The church, once a sanctuary of peace, had now become a witness to violence and fear. And as the sounds of the ambulance faded into the distance, new questions began to take root in the minds of those left behind: *Why Father Landry? And would they ever feel safe here again?* The events of that day were still too fresh, too raw, to fully comprehend. But one thing was certain—the city had changed. And Father Landry, perhaps one of its most trusted symbols of hope and guidance, was now clinging to life, caught in the wake of a violent and unpredictable force that no one seemed able to stop.

The once hallowed space, filled with the soft murmurs of prayer just hours before, now buzzed with tension and disbelief. Locals from the surrounding neighborhood started showing up to see what was happening. The church began to fill with spectators. A woman, her hands trembling, stood up slowly from her kneeling position, glancing around the room. She had been closest to Father Landry when the attack occurred and had seen the look of pain and confusion in his eyes as the hooded figure struck him down. Her breath hitched as she tried to make sense of the horror, but words failed her. "Why?" she murmured, her voice barely audible, as she turned to the man beside her, whose face was ashen with fear. "How could he... how could anyone do this to him?" the man responded; his words thick with disbelief. He was holding his rosary, his fingers nervously running over the beads, as if seeking comfort in the familiar object. "Father Landry... he's always been... always been a good man. A good priest. Why would anyone—"

"Is he dead?" another parishioner interrupted, her voice cutting through the conversation. Her face was pale, and her hands gripped the back of a pew as though it were the only thing keeping her from collapsing. "Is he dead?" she asked again, her voice rising in panic.

"No," the first man replied, though his own voice faltered. "They said he was alive... for now. They're taking him to the hospital." But even as he said it, there was a sense of dread hanging over his words. No one could say for certain if Father Landry would survive. Not after an attack like that. Around them, hushed conversations began to spiral into more frantic murmurs. Every person in the church seemed to have their own theory about the Vindicator. The vigilante, once regarded with a twisted sense of admiration for his violent form of justice, was beginning to be seen in a different light entirely. The attack on Father Landry had shattered any remaining illusion that the Vindicator was simply a man fighting for good. His

## CHAPTER 8: BLASPHEMOUS TONGUE

violent assault on a priest—a figure who represented everything good and pure in the city—was a line no one had expected him to cross.

"He's no hero," a middle-aged woman muttered under her breath as she clutched her purse to her chest. "He's a monster. A monster hiding under a hood."

A man near the front of the church, shaking his head in disbelief, added, "I don't know what to believe anymore. I thought he was taking out criminals, you know? People who deserved it. But a priest? This is... this is something else."

The murmurs grew louder, the confusion and anger mounting with every passing moment. Some were angry at the Vindicator for what he had done, others at the authorities for not stopping him sooner. But there were also whispers of fear—fear of what would possibly happen next. Could the Vindicator be coming for them, too? Could no one hide from him? No one was safe, not anymore.

Amid the chaos, one elderly man stood up, his voice trembling but determined as he made his way toward the altar. He was dressed in a long overcoat, with his hands shaking as he clutched his Bible tightly to his chest. He took a few faltering steps toward the front of the church, the noise of the congregation swirling around him, until he reached the pulpit. There, he turned to face the crowd, his face drawn but resolute.

"We must pray," he said, his voice rising above the din of the voices. "We must pray for Father Landry and for this city of ours. The Vindicator may strike again, but our faith will carry us through."

A few of the parishioners, those still clinging to their faith, nodded slowly, the words offering a small measure of comfort. But many others remained frozen, their minds still spinning in disbelief. They had come to church seeking peace, and now they were faced with a reality where that peace no longer existed.

The elderly man continued, "This is a test, brothers and sisters. A test of our faith. Do not let fear overtake us. Do not let this act of violence strip us of what makes us human—our compassion, our hope."

But his words were drowned out by the growing chorus of anxiety. Someone in the back shouted, "What if he comes for us next?"

The room erupted in a flood of voices, the fear that had once been silent now spilling into open panic. People moved toward the doors, some stumbling as they rushed to leave, others clutching their loved ones tightly. They sought an escape from the suffocating dread that had descended upon the church. Like a fog of uncertainty that had descended on the city. The Vindicator's shadow loomed large over them all, and no one knew who would be next.

The news of the unbelievable attack spread like wildfire through the city, carried by frantic whispers and urgent conversations in the streets. As the details of what had transpired in the church reached more and more ears, a deep, unsettling fear began to settle over the populace. People rushed to spread the word, their voices trembling with disbelief, yet tinged with a growing sense of dread. What had once been considered a vague and distant threat in the form of the Vindicator was now an undeniable and harsh reality—one that shook the very foundations of the city's sense of safety. The attack on the priest was a stark reminder of the power and ruthlessness of this enigmatic figure. The horror of it sent ripples through every corner of the city, unsettling even the most hardened citizens. A profound sense of unease took an even stronger hold of the streets. The once semi-peaceful city was now gripped by a pervasive anxiety, as if the very air had changed. Peo-

## CHAPTER 8: BLASPHEMOUS TONGUE

ple moved with even more caution, their eyes darting nervously to every shadow, every alley. These attacks were no longer distributed by just a shadowy figure who delivered swift punishment to criminals; his scope had broadened, and now, even those who had once been considered beyond reproach—men of the cloth, symbols of piety and sanctity—were not even safe from his wrath.

There was now even more of a growing confusion over the Vindicator's true nature. With the tragic death of the prostitute, and now this brutal assault on a respected priest, the question had shifted from whether he was a vigilante, to whether he could even still be considered one. His actions were becoming increasingly hard to justify as anything other than violent, indiscriminate punishment. Where once people might have sympathized with his mission—however brutal it may have been—there was now an undeniable shift in sentiment. The very notion of him as a protagonist seemed more fragile with some of these new acts of violence. What had morphed into a murky morally gray area was now bleeding into a much more sinister place. Was the Vindicator truly serving justice, or was he now, simply a man, drunk on power, wielding violence without conscience?

The public's perception of the Vindicator had changed. The line between right and wrong was no longer so clear-cut. The people's trust in the city's safety crumbled further. There were whispers in the taverns, in the marketplaces, and in the alleys, questions that once seemed irrelevant now coming to the forefront: *What will become of this city? How much longer before we're all living in fear of this man, no matter where we go?* His violent spree was leaving more than just physical scars on the city; it was eroding away any sense of peace and order that still existed. Would anyone ever feel truly safe again? Or had the city's fate already been sealed?

## CHAPTER 9: POLICY OF PUNISHMENT

Baptiste and Foret had barely heard the full transmission over their police scanner when the adrenaline instantly kicked in. The call was brief but urgent—something about a violent incident at St. Patrick's Church, and a priest being targeted. Baptiste exchanged a quick look with Foret, before both detectives scrambled into action. There was no time to waste. They each grabbed their gear—their guns, radio, and a flashlight—and the two of them bolted out of the precinct, their boots hitting the pavement in a hurried rhythm. The possibility that Father Landry could be the victim sent a chill down Baptiste's spine. The well-known priest had been a vocal advocate for his community, doing his part to end the Vindicator's reign of terror.

The city streets blurred as they made their way to the historic church. It was only a few blocks from the precinct, but the air felt thick with urgency, and every second seemed to stretch. As they neared St. Patrick's, they saw the slew of flashing lights of patrol

## CHAPTER 9: POLICY OF PUNISHMENT

cars and other first responders clogging the streets. The scene was already chaotic, with witnesses and parishioners huddled together, eyes wide with confusion and fear. The officers had erected a perimeter, pushing the growing crowd back from the church's entrance. The detectives weaved their way through the onlookers, instinctively scanning the area for any sign of the priest or better yet, the suspect. Baptiste's heart raced as she spotted a group of distraught women near the entrance, weeping softly.

Baptiste, ever the level-headed one, was quick to seek information. She approached a group of parishioners asking about Father Landry and his whereabouts. They soon learn that the horrifically injured priest had left for the hospital and is in what appeared to be pretty bad shape. Baptiste and Foret exchanged their well-known uneasy glances as they stood in the midst of the confusion around the historic church. They gathered what information they could from the depressed witnesses. From what they learned, everything pointed to the same conclusion: the anonymous parishioner who had confessed the day before was likely the same person responsible for the violent attack on Father Landry. The details of the confession haunted Baptiste's mind—the man had been agitated, desperate, and fearful. And now, here they were, facing the aftermath of that same desperation, the bloodshed echoing in the hollow silence of the church. It couldn't just be a coincidence. The dots were connecting, but they needed more than assumptions—they needed confirmation from Father Landry himself.

Before they could reach him, they had to gather what additional information they could. The detectives split up, moving among the few witnesses who hadn't fled in terror when the attack occurred, and were still there to aid the investigators in any way they could. Most of the congregation had been in a state of shock, but a few had managed to stay calm enough to provide some exact details. The parishioners were shaken, their faces pale and drained as they recounted the moments of horror. The older woman at the front of the group had seen a man lurking near the altar just before the violence erupted. Another witness, a young man who had been kneeling in prayer, described hearing raised voices—pleas, perhaps, or threats—before the unmistakable sound of a struggle. It all seemed to fit the description of the man who had confessed to Landry the day before, but they needed to know for sure.

Baptiste listened intently, piecing together the fragments of the story while jotting down notes in her notebook. But there was one thing that didn't sit right with her: the attacker's motives were still unclear. *Why had he targeted Father Landry in the first place? Was it an act of revenge for speaking to the department? A personal vendetta? Or was it some deep and twisted belief that had driven him to this violence?* She didn't have the answers yet, but the growing certainty that yesterday's awkward confession was tied to the attack fueled her determination. They needed to find Landry, get his account of the events, and confirm whether this was definitely the same man who had come to him in need of absolution.

Foret, meanwhile, was collecting additional descriptions of the assailant. Several witnesses had seen the attacker—though in the chaos, their recollections varied. Some described a tall man with a gaunt face, his features obscured by a hood, while others mentioned a shorter, stockier build. But one detail remained consistent: the man's eyes. Descriptions of them were eerily similar—dark, hollow, like they belonged to someone who had lost touch with reality. It was the kind of description that haunted you, stayed with you long after the encounter. Baptiste couldn't help but think of the confession from the day before. Landry had spoken

## CHAPTER 9: POLICY OF PUNISHMENT

of those same haunted eyes, the same fearful tone in the man's voice. It all felt like a thread waiting to be pulled, the answers just out of reach.

As they finished up their interviews with the witnesses, the scene at St. Patrick's Church was slowly starting to calm. The initial shock had begun to wear off, and the crowd that had gathered outside was finally thinning out. The murmurs of concern, fear, and speculation had quieted, replaced by the dull sounds of conversation and the occasional scrape of shoes against the gravel courtyard. Baptiste could feel the weight of this latest twist pressing down on her—unanswered questions, too many uncertainties—and the urgency to piece it all together distressed her.

Foret was scribbling down a few last details from a parishioner when a figure caught Zoe's attention. She noticed him first—a tall, pale man walking across the church courtyard at a relaxed pace, his features angular and sharp. His eyes were fixed on Pete, and for a moment, Zoe felt a strange chill. The man's gaze never wavered, locking in with Pete's as he moved through the crowd. Zoe couldn't shake the feeling that the two of them were engaged in some sort of silent exchange, an unspoken understanding that seemed to stretch out longer than usual. It wasn't the casual glance that one would expect in passing; it felt like a deliberate moment of connection, something charged, though neither of them made any outward move to acknowledge it.

Zoe's attention stayed on them as the man's gaze finally broke. He allowed a subtle smirk to tug at the corner of his lips before turning and continuing his walk, blending back into the crowd as if nothing had happened. Strangely, he was barely affected by all the chaotic factors laid out before him. He never looked around at the large crime scene with curiosity once, as he focused on Pete.

It was a fleeting moment, but Zoe couldn't shake the unease it left in her stomach. There had been something about the way the two of them locked their eyes, something that felt more intimate than a mere passing coincidence. She turned her focus back to Pete, who was still talking to a witness, though she could sense that the encounter had slightly affected him too, even if he wasn't showing it.

She couldn't let it go. Once Pete finished his last conversation, Zoe stepped closer, her brow furrowed.

"Hey," she said, trying to keep her tone casual, "That guy a friend of yours?"

Pete looked at her quickly, the question catching him off guard. His face softened, but there was an edge to his response. "No. Not at all. Why?"

Zoe tilted her head slightly, studying him. She tried to read his expression, which was calm, but there was a flicker in his eyes, something she couldn't quite place.

"Oh, it just seemed like a longer than normal interaction," she said, her voice light but probing. "Almost like you may have known him, you know? You two kind of locked in on each other for a while there."

Pete shrugged, brushing it off with an easy, almost rehearsed smile.

"Nah. I don't know him. Never seen him before. Just... I don't know, felt like an uneasy vibe as he passed by. Nothing major."

Zoe wasn't convinced, but she let it go. Pete's calm exterior made it hard to read him, and she didn't want to push it further, not with everything else they still had to focus on. Even though the scene outside the church was starting to quiet down, they still had plenty of work to do. She simply nodded, though the moment lingered in her mind. There was something about that exchange that felt off, but Zoe knew better than jumping to conclusions, especially without more information.

Pete, for his part, didn't seem troubled by the encounter, though Zoe couldn't help but wonder if there was more to it than he was letting on. The man's expression—the way he had smirked at Pete before walking away—it had seemed so deliberate. But if Pete wasn't concerned, Zoe didn't want to press it. There were bigger questions to answer now. The attack on Father Landry obviously was still the priority. They needed answers, and they needed them fast.

With that, they both returned to their work, but Zoe kept the image of the pale man in her mind, watching the crowds with a new sense of wariness. Something about the way he had passed in front of the crime scene, so deliberately, stuck with her. It felt like an omen—an unsettling hint that they were on the verge of uncovering something darker than they could have imagined.

As she is putting her gear in the squad car, Zoe began to realize that the man who had locked eyes with Pete... he did kind of fit the confessor's description, at least in part. There was that eerie calmness about him, an immovable confidence that Zoe couldn't shake. It was just like Landry had described. If this relaxed onlooker could be the confessor, he didn't seem afraid, or even concerned about the presence of the police. Something that most suspects in a high-profile case like this would have. Instead, he just moved through the crowd with a kind of detached ease, as if he knew exactly where he was going and who he was looking at. Pete had mentioned the uneasy vibe he felt as the man passed, but Zoe felt like there was more to it. It wasn't just the man's presence that unsettled Pete. It was the interaction itself. Could it have been him?

Could this pale, tall man be the actual Vindicator, the one responsible for the string of attacks that had sent shockwaves through the city? And if so, was he the same man from the confession or from today's brutal assault? If so, he wasn't just any criminal—he was a methodical, calculated individual, someone who saw himself as a purifier, a force of righteous fury. Father Landry had been attacked, but this attack seemed more personal—it was targeted, even more than some of the others. And this man, this stranger that was not concealed in any way, who had locked eyes with Pete and had acted far too calm, too controlled.... Could he be the attacker?

Zoe's thoughts raced as she pieced her rampant thoughts together. The Vindicator's attacks had all shared a disturbing pattern, an almost ritualistic quality, an element of theatricality. They weren't random acts of violence; they were deliberate statements, each one meant to send a clear message. Father Landry's injury wasn't just about violence—it was also a symbol, a calculated strike. And Zoe had a creeping suspicion that whoever had done this wasn't done yet. She scanned the perimeter repeatedly looking for the strange man, but he had disappeared. *If only she would've stop him for questioning sooner.* Her eyes flicked over to Pete, who was still speaking with another witness, but her mind wasn't on the case at hand anymore. The more she thought about it, the more she realized that the person they had just seen didn't feel like just an innocent bystander passing through the scene. He had been watching Pete, sizing him up, or maybe even testing him. Zoe felt the weight of something heavy settling over her. *Was the Vindicator just here? Was he trying to send a message of his elusiveness, or even worse, possibly targeting one of them working too closely on his case?*

She glanced over at Pete again, the flickering doubt beginning to shift into certainty. She knew her partner. Pete was no stranger

## CHAPTER 9: POLICY OF PUNISHMENT

to the bizarre, to the dangerous, and to the unsettling. He had been through too many high-stakes cases to let his guard down so easily. But this moment—this brief exchange he had with this man—it had slightly rattled him in a way that was impossible to totally ignore. Pete was tough, but something about that man had gotten under his skin.

Now, as they prepared to leave, she was the one who couldn't shake the feeling that they were being watched, that someone was always one step ahead, pulling the strings from the shadows. She now knew about these same feelings that Father had spoken of during their last meeting. If the Vindicator was already aware of them—if he had been so close—then they were playing a dangerous game. Zoe's instincts were telling her that they had just crossed the point of no return. The Vindicator was close, and he had to be watching.

She took a slow breath and turned back to Pete, who had just finished speaking with a witness and was moving toward her. He seemed mostly unaffected, but she saw the tension in his eyes—the flicker of unease he hadn't quite managed to hide. She wasn't the only one who had felt it. As Pete approached, she knew the moment for casual dismissals had passed.

"We need to talk," she said quietly, her voice sharp with urgency. Pete looked at her, his expression unreadable.

"About what?" he asked, but Zoe could see the concern starting to settle in behind his eyes.

"The guy. The one who just passed through our crime scene like he was on a chipper Sunday stroll without a care in the world. I think we need to keep an eye out for him, and look a little deeper if we do catch up with him. I don't think it's just a coincidence," Zoe said, her voice low but steady. "He could be our guy. You know how some of these weirdos like to come back to the scene as a spectator to get their rocks off again."

"Which guy?" he responds. "The Vindicator, the confessor, today's attacker, or the Sunday stroll guy?"

"That's just it, Pete. He could be all four!"

Pete's eyes narrowed slightly in surprise as he glanced around the courtyard. He didn't speak right away, but the silence between them spoke volumes. Zoe wasn't sure if Pete was ready to accept it, but she felt in her gut that she was right.

"That's pretty ballsy on his part, don't you' think?" he finally responds. "I mean if that was him, he actually just waltzed through here and not one of the witnesses recognized him?"

"I know, he's either brave or stupid." She adds, "Remember, most people didn't see his face due to him being covered up."

"Yeah, I guess, but damn." he adds.

Pete just shrugged his shoulders as he scanned the area once more. Something about that man told Zoe that they were dealing with far more than they had first thought. They were going to have to be more careful and detailed than ever. They were closer to the truth than they realized. And that truth was far darker than anything either of them had imagined. If he got to Landry, they could conceivably be next on his list. And they'd be waiting.

Later that evening, as the sky darkened, and the hospital hummed with the usual late-night activity, Zoe and Pete received an update. An officer stationed at the hospital called in to inform them that Father Landry had successfully made it through surgery and was now recovering in the ICU. The priest was stable, but still unconscious, though the doctors were hopeful he would wake soon enough to answer some questions. They could finally get some crucial details about the attack, or so they thought.

## CHAPTER 9: POLICY OF PUNISHMENT

However, there was an unsettling twist. The officer mentioned, almost casually, that Landry wouldn't be able to speak when he regained consciousness.

"You'll need a notebook," the officer continued, "because unfortunately, he won't be talking to anyone. The attacker... cut out his tongue."

The detectives were both taken aback by the brutal detail. The violence of the assault had just escalated in their minds. Not only had the priest been attacked, but the deliberate mutilation—removing his ability to speak—spoke volumes about the sadistic nature of the attacker. The situation was more dire than they had realized, and they both understood now, more than ever, the magnitude of who they were dealing with.

The next morning, the air in the hospital felt heavier as Zoe and Pete walked down the sterile, quiet hallways toward Father Landry's recovery room. The smell of antiseptic and the distant beeping of monitors filled the space, but all they could think about was their favorite priest. What he might relay once he awoke, and what new revelations might come to light.

When they entered his room, Landry was groggy, but awake, his eyes flickering toward them. His face was pale, his eyes tired but sharp, the weight of his ordeal still heavy on his features, with bandages wrapped around his neck and mouth. Despite the pain in his appearance, there was a kind of calm acceptance in his expression. His hands were resting on the bed, and as Zoe and Pete approached, he reached out and held each of their hands simultaneously, his slight smile hidden beneath the gauze and wraps on his face. He reaches for a small notepad and pen on the bedside table. With a slight nod to acknowledge their presence, Landry scribbled down something quickly, then held it up for them to see. His writing was shaky but legible. *It was him. The same man from yesterday's confession. He came back for me.*

Zoe's heart skipped a beat as she read the words. She looked at Pete, who met her gaze, his expression mirroring the realization that had just hit them both: they weren't just dealing with any random criminal. Father Landry's attacker—the one who had left him in this state—was none other than the infamous Vindicator. Zoe was right, her gut feelings had been true. She leaned closer; her voice was low but urgent. "Can you write down what happened, Father? What did he say to you?"

Landry's teary eyes darkened, and he began writing again, his hand trembling slightly. *He said I was part of the corruption. That I was just like the others. I begged him to stop, but...* Landry's eyes flickered, and he paused, swallowing hard as if the memory of the man's words was too much to bear. He slowly lifted the pen again, finishing the note with a few final words. *He cut me to silence me, to make sure I couldn't speak out, like I was a blasphemer. He believes the world is better without people who try to stop him from doing the Lord's work. He wants people to get out of his way and let him save whomever he can.*

The gravity of Landry's message settled over them like a heavy weight. The Vindicator wasn't just targeting priests indiscriminately—he had chosen Landry for a reason, and that reason was the warped sense of justice they had come to know so well. The priest wasn't just a random victim of violence; he had been marked by the Vindicator for what he represented: a symbol of false authority and, in the attacker's eyes, corruption that was against him and God's plan. Baptiste clenched her jaw, her mind racing once again. The heat was about to get turned up a notch, as the hunt for the Vindicator had just become even more urgent—and most

## CHAPTER 9: POLICY OF PUNISHMENT

assuredly, more dangerous.

There was one more critical piece of information that Father Landry had to share with Zoe and Pete, a revelation that had come to him in the fog of his recovery. Over the last twelve hours, as he drifted in and out of consciousness, the priest had experienced something that he could only describe as a vision—an epiphany that broke through the haze of pain and disorientation. It was the name, the attacker's last name. At first, the details had been hazy, but the more Landry thought about it, the clearer it became. He recalled that, during his time as a priest, he had met the man on a few occasions after mass. The man had sought his counsel, confiding in him about struggles and doubts. It was during these few sessions that Landry had remembered seeing on the donation envelopes that the man had submitted for the poor box, there it was: his name. And in that moment of clarity, Landry knew. The man who had attacked him was someone he had once known, someone whose name he had never truly forgotten. It was just buried in the back of his mind, released now from his present condition.

Landry grabbed the notepad again, his hand shaking slightly more, as he scrawled down the name with urgency. Breaux—he was certain of it. It was the last name, but the first name was still somewhat of a mystery. He had seen the name on the donation envelopes, but he couldn't recall whether it was Mike, Mark, or Matt. All he knew was that the man's last name was Breaux. His heart raced as he continued to write. *If I had to guess, I'd say Mark was the first name. That feels the most right.* He handed the notebook to Zoe and Pete, his eyes filled with a mixture of hope and exhaustion.

The detectives exchanged looks, their excitement intense. The name "Breaux" was like a key that had just unlocked a door in their minds. It was a breakthrough, a tangible lead they could finally chase down. For months, the Vindicator had terrorized the city, and now they were closer than ever to possibly unmasking him. Zoe's mind raced with possibilities—there were likely records of donations, maybe even a history of the Breaux family living in the area. They were finally narrowing in on the notorious criminal. It felt like the walls were closing in on their hated attacker, and for the first time in weeks, they could feel the pressure building on the man who had eluded them for so long.

This wasn't just a clue; it was a lifeline. The detectives knew they had to act fast. They finally had a name. Now they needed to move, to track down every lead, every possible connection. Mike or Mark Breaux, or whichever first name he went by, was about to become the focus of their investigation, and Zoe and Pete were determined to bring him to justice before he could strike again. The net was closing in, and they would not let him slip away again.

Feeling recharged by the new lead, Zoe and Pete left the hospital and returned to the precinct, their minds buzzing with anticipation. They knew the real work was just beginning. The detective team wasted no time diving into the station's database to sift through records, cross-referencing every possible lead that might connect the name "M. Breaux" to their suspect. The process was slow and methodical, fueled by hours of research and analysis, but they were determined to work through the exhaustion. One by one, they eliminated potential candidates, narrowing the list down as they dug deeper into each Breaux's background. The more they uncovered, the more certain they became. Mark Breaux was their man.

Breaux's address put him right in the heart of the area where most of the attacks had occurred. The few neighbors who had known him spoke of him in low, wary tones. He was described as a reclusive hermit—someone who rarely left his home, who kept to himself and hardly interacted with anyone. This fit perfectly with the sparse details from the witnesses who had seen the Vindicator in action, or fleeing from the crime scenes. His drab, nondescript appearance, often blending into the background, matched the descriptions of the attacker given by those few who had glimpsed him. A quiet man, withdrawn, almost invisible in the day-to-day hustle of the city. It was starting to add up in ways they hadn't expected, but it was all pointing in one direction: Mark Breaux had to be the Vindicator.

After exhausting every lead and running through every possible scenario, Zoe and Pete finally felt the thrill of certainty. It was time to act. Father Landry had been released from the hospital and was now recovering at home, in the rectory. The detectives, eager to move forward, paid him a visit to let him know they had zeroed in on their prime suspect, while checking on the new security system that was recently installed as well. They arrived at the rectory to visit Landry. He looked far better than he had in the hospital, and he welcomed them in with a tired but grateful smile. They sat down with him, the weight of the moment hanging dense in the air.

"Hello Father, we've narrowed it down to one," Pete said, his voice calm but tinged with excitement. "Mark Breaux. We need you to take a look at something."

Zoe pulled out a folder containing a small lineup of photos, each image carefully selected from their search of local records. They spread the photos across the table in front of Father Landry, who leaned forward, squinting at the faces in front of him. His fingers lightly brushed the edge of the folder, as though he was bracing himself for what he might see. The moment felt surreal—finally here they were, one step away from identifying the Vindicator, the man who had attacked not only the priest they loved but terrorized the entire city for months.

Zoe says gently, "Father, we just need you to look at these photos. Take your time. If you see anyone you recognize, someone who might be him, we need to know."

Landry nods, his eyes scanning each photograph slowly, deliberately. His gaze lingered on each one, his brow furrowed in concentration. For a moment, there was silence. Then, with a soft exhale, he stops at one photo, his finger tapping gently against it. His eyes widen and he grunts in affirmation while pointing to the last photo.

Zoe and Pete exchanged a look, and the feeling that had been building inside them—a sense of inevitability—now solidified into something far more tangible. They finally had their man. The detectives gathered the photos and stood to leave, the weight of the case suddenly feeling both lighter and heavier at the same time. They had the identity of the vaunted Vindicator, but the real work was just beginning. They needed to move hastily, just in case Breaux might try to disappear into the shadows once again, like he had done so many times before. But for the first time in weeks, they could finally see the light at the end of the dark tunnel. The Vindicator was no longer just a phantom in the dark. They had a name, a face, and the next step was clear: they had to bring him in before he could strike again.

The excitement that everyone had was tempered after a new breaking update on the case had just come in. One of the detective's fellow deputies called Baptiste on her cell phone to explain what had just transpired. She pauses and puts her cell on speaker for Pete and Landry to listen in as well. The unknown officer continues with the surprising update. Two eyewitnesses

CHAPTER 9: POLICY OF PUNISHMENT 133

had stumbled upon the Vindicator seemingly caught in the act of punishing a known child sex offender! The whole city knew of this child predator, because of the local mailout cards being sent to the neighborhoods, exposing his prior dirty deeds. He was being integrated back into society after serving jail time, but he would forever be listed on the child sex predator list as part of his parole.

This predator had been the apparent next targeted victim to be punished or vindicated, and he had just been apprehended down by the old, abandoned Pontchartrain Beach area at the New Orleans Lake Front. The Vindicator evidently had been caught in the middle of the latest of his radical acts of atonement. His victim, the child predator, had sustained a broken leg, courtesy of his kidnapper. He was obviously heavily intoxicated and had a large cinder block chained around his neck as well. He was incoherent and lying in the surf of the popular lake's beachhead. The Vindicator had hastily dropped him after being interrupted by two transient types that were passing by and noticed the Vindicator dragging the man from his car to the water's edge. When they yelled for the hooded man to stop what he was doing, he dropped the injured victim, jumped in the predator's vehicle and sped off.

Baptiste puzzled, thanks the officer and hangs up. She asks aloud, "Why the hell did he have a block chained around his neck?"

Foret replies, "That's weird, but I'm going with a possible future drowning victim. But if so, why? He would've had another possible death on his hands. That really isn't his thing. Or maybe he's starting to like killing a little more than just marring people now. Like, maybe he's become the grim reaper, instead of just a religious fanatic trying to 'save' people?"

Father Landry, after pausing in deep thought, gestures to them after writing down a phrase on his notepad: *Matthew 18: 6-9.*

Baptiste hurriedly looks around the room for one of Father's closest bibles. She hands it to Landry, and he pages through the book and right to the Gospel of Matthew. He nods his head, and hands the book to Baptiste, and Foret joins her as they read the following excerpt: *"If anyone causes one of these little ones- those who believe in me- to stumble, it would be better for them to have a large millstone hung around their neck and to drown in the depths of the sea. Woe to the world because of the things that cause people to stumble! Such things must come, but woe to the person through whom they come! If your hand or your foot causes you to stumble, cut it off and throw it away. It is better for you to enter life, maimed or crippled, than to have two hands or two feet and be thrown into eternal fire."*

# CHAPTER 10: THE NET CLOSES IN

The moment they had all been waiting for had finally arrived. After months of meticulous planning, countless hours spent combing through evidence, and an ever-growing sense of urgency, the time to strike had come. With a warrant in hand, the detectives gathered in the department's briefing room, their faces set with determination. This was the culmination of weeks of intense work, and now they were ready to bring down one of the most elusive suspects they had ever tracked. The atmosphere in the room was charged with anticipation as the team prepared for their final plan of attack.

Captain Leclair stood at the head of the table, the chalkboard behind him covered in scribbles and maps that outlined the operation in painstaking detail. He looked over the room and nodded to his team. The plan had been carefully crafted, and everyone had a specific role to play. The briefing was short and to the point, yet every word held weight. The target was Mark Breaux, a man who had proven to be the Vindicator. His last known residence was an apartment on the outskirts of the French Quarter, a place that had become his hidden fortress in recent months.

The team's focus shifted as Leclair spoke again, this time singling out the two officers who had led the charge from the start.

"Baptiste and Foret," the captain spoke aloud, his voice steady but firm.

"You two are going in on point. You've put in the most time and effort tracking this bastard down. You've earned the right to be at the tip of the spear."

The room went quiet for a moment, the weight of the responsibility settling on their shoulders. Baptiste and Foret exchanged a glance, the unspoken understanding between them visible. Many of their fellow officers gave them unspoken positive head nods and clenched fists, reinforcing Leclair's statement. They had been working tirelessly on this case for months, following the trail of breadcrumbs Breaux had left behind. They had poured over countless hours of surveillance footage, gathered intelligence from informants, and done everything in their power to close in on him. Now, with all of their hard work, it was all coming to a proverbial head.

With the conclusion of the briefing and the final plan laid out, the team set their minds to the momentous task at hand. An undercover officer had been keeping a close watch on Breaux's apartment, reporting back with timely updates. The green light had been given from the top, signaling that now was the time to move. The air outside was heavy with the humid late afternoon heat, but inside the station, the focus was sharp. Each member of the team moved swiftly and with purpose, double-checking their gear, confirming their positions, and preparing themselves mentally for what was to come. The knowledge that Breaux was a dangerous man, capable of anything to avoid capture, made the stakes even higher. There was no room for error.

As Baptiste and Foret geared up, the adrenaline began to rise. Their hearts beat faster, but there was no room for nerves, only precision and professionalism. They had been in high-stakes situations before, but this one was different. This wasn't just about catching a criminal. It was about putting an end to a reign of terror that had plagued their beloved city. They knew Breaux had managed to slip through their fingers on numerous occasions, but this time they were confident they had him cornered. The detective duo had become familiar with the rhythms of the French Quarter and its surrounding streets, and though Breaux was known to be unpredictable, they had carefully studied his patterns. They knew he was smart and dangerous, but the element of surprise was on their side.

The unit, now fully mobilized, moved in a coordinated fashion, each officer responsible for shutting down traffic and forcing bystanders inside of buildings. They then took their reinforcing assigned positions as they approached the outer streets of the apartment building. There was no turning back now. The time to act was upon them, and the city's streets were about to bear witness to the culmination of their relentless pursuit.

The main assault team arrived at the staging area around the corner from the target's home, their vehicles gliding to a stop with military precision. Without a word, they began to disembark, the sound of doors clicking open and boots hitting the pavement muffled by the thick, humid air of the evening. Every officer knew exactly where they needed to be, and they moved quickly, and quietly—just as they had rehearsed countless times before. They fanned out in all directions, positioning themselves with calculated efficiency to surround the suspect's domicile. Each member of the team was a piece of a larger puzzle, strategically placed to eliminate any possible escape route for the suspect, Mark Breaux. They moved with the ease of a well-rehearsed dance, spreading out slowly and methodically in front of the double apartment's front porch. There was a certain grace to their movements—precise, deliberate, almost choreographed, like a beautiful but deadly waltz. In a way, it was almost beautiful, but there was nothing romantic about it. This was an operation months in the making, and every officer had a role to play. The entire team moved with predator-like precision, silently inching closer to their unaware target. The air around them dense, charged with anticipation. They weren't just catching a hunted suspect; it was about ending this dangerous cat and mouse game that had gone on for far too long. They were laser focused and ready. It was time to gain some credibility back for their ridiculed department as well.

At the forefront of the team, Lead Detective Pete Foret stood with his eyes fixed on the apartment's door. The years of experience and countless operations had honed his senses to a razor's edge. Baptiste, his attractive yet deliberate partner, was by his side, her posture equally tense but steady. Foret caught her eye for just a split second, his face cracking into a slight grin, one that conveyed a mix of determination and a deep familiarity with the moment. Without a word, he winked at her—an almost imperceptible gesture, but one that was understood between them. A shared look that said, *we've got this*. It was a moment of silent reassurance, one of those small gestures that carried weight in high-stress situations like this. Then, the moment passed. Foret's grin faded into seriousness, and he immediately turned to the task at hand. He

## CHAPTER 10: THE NET CLOSES IN

stepped forward to the apartment door, his movements swift but controlled. He drew his pistol, the weapon held low but ready. The only sound now was the soft rustling of uniforms and the occasional murmur of the other officers as they took their positions around the building. Foret raised his hand and slammed it against the door with authority, his voice carrying over the stillness.

"Police, open up!" His words were sharp, commanding, and filled with the weight of authority.

But as his voice echoed through the building, there was nothing—no sound, no movement. Just silence. The kind of silence that made the hairs on the back of your neck stand on end. Pete's gaze never wavered, his eyes scanning the shadows beyond the door, waiting for a sign of life, anything. But nothing. He knocked again. This time with even more force, making sure the impact echoed louder, carrying the gravity of the situation.

"Open up, Mr. Breaux! It's the NOPD, and we know you're in there!" His voice rang out again, louder this time, more insistent.

"Open up and come out with your hands up, or we will be forced to kick the door down!"

Still, there was no response. Again, no movement from inside the apartment. Foret's expression hardened as his patience began to wear thin. This was not the first time they had run into silence like this, but the stakes were much higher on this one.

He stepped back slightly and shouted once more, his voice lower, more controlled, but there was a clear edge to it. "This is your last warning, Mark! Come out with your hands where we can see them! Don't make us come in there!"

The weight of the warning hung in the air. He knew Breaux was there. Everything had led them to this moment. But still, no movement. No sound. The seconds stretched on, heavy with expectation. Foret's jaw clenched. It was the kind of silence that spoke volumes, and every instinct in his body told him that Breaux was not going to cooperate. Foret exchanged a quick glance with Baptiste, her eyes narrowing in silent understanding. This was it. The moment they had been waiting for was now. There would be no further warnings. They had done everything by the book, and now it was time. Could he have killed himself inside, knowing that he was finally caught? They were about to find out, one way or the other.

Baptiste's hand subtly moved, a quick signal to the team, and in an instant, the atmosphere shifted a notch again. The strike team was crisp and ready to pounce. Foret stepped back, his fingers tightening around the grip of his weapon. It was clear—if alive, Breaux wasn't going to come out peacefully. They would have to go in and flush him or carry him out. The operation had stalled enough, and the door would be coming down momentarily. And once it did, there would be no place for Breaux to hide. Just like his victims were helpless, he would now be the same.

After a tense pause, Baptiste's gaze locked onto the door one last time before her fingers twitched, signaling the team. It was the moment they had been waiting for, the moment when patience turned into action. Her eyes briefly met Foret's, and with a subtle but decisive motion, she gave the final hand signal—quick, sharp, and unmistakable. The team was in position, and there was no turning back now. Her voice cut through the stillness with a low growl: "Fuck it, it's gametime."

The words were more than just a command; they were the green light that set everything in motion. Instantly, a large officer, a hulking figure with a broad chest and arms thick as tree trunks, stepped forward. Clutching a heavy metal battering ram, he ap-

## CHAPTER 10: THE NET CLOSES IN

proached the apartment's door with the kind of resolve that comes only from years of experience in high-pressure situations. The first strike landed with a deafening crash that shook the door on its hinges, splintering the wood with brutal force. A second strike followed, harder, more violent, and this time, the door gave way completely. It was a moment of awesome destruction, the culmination of months of preparation and tense waiting.

Without hesitation, Baptiste and Foret rushed forward, moving as one, guns drawn, ready for anything. The tension was thick, and the sound of their footsteps echoed in the narrow hallway as they barreled through the threshold of the apartment. They were first through the smashed door, a well-rehearsed duo, both their weapons raised and scanning the dimly lit space for any sign of movement. Behind them, the rest of the team flowed in like orchestrated lights, covering their backs and securing each room with methodical precision.

They moved through the apartment with flawless coordination, every turn and step in perfect harmony. The years of working together had made them almost like a single organism, their movements instinctive, honed to perfection. They didn't need to communicate with words; each one knew their role in the operation, and each step brought them closer to the target. The apartment had an eerie stillness, as though it was holding its breath, waiting for the long-awaited confrontation to unfold. Baptiste's senses were sharp, every detail in the room, every sound, registering in her mind. It wasn't just training that had brought them to this point, it was the trust they had in one another, the unspoken bond between them and the rest of the team.

As they moved through the main hallway, Baptiste's mind raced with superior efficiency. They had cleared the living area, checked the kitchen, and now they were heading for the back of the apartment. It didn't take long before they reached the final room, the master bedroom. The door was ajar, and there, kneeling in the middle of the room, was Mark Breaux. He seemed to be lost in thought, his eyes closed, his head slightly bowed. Around him, scattered on the floor, were several empty liquor bottles, evidence of his last attempts to drown whatever demons plagued him.

The sight caught Baptiste somewhat off guard. For a moment, it was almost surreal, like something out of a twisted movie. Breaux was a man who had evaded capture for so long, and yet here he was before them, the mighty Vindicator, seemingly vulnerable, caught in a moment of weakness. But Baptiste didn't let her guard down. They had him cornered, but she knew Breaux was dangerous, he had to be. No one survived this long on the run without being cunning and ruthless.

"Get up! Slowly!" Baptiste commanded, her voice firm but controlled.

"Hands up! Now!" Foret's voice cut through the air, its usual calm now laced with the tension of the situation.

They weren't about to let him make a move that could turn deadly. Breaux opened his eyes slowly, blinking as though coming out of a daze. His gaze immediately fixed on Foret, and to Baptiste's surprise, an unusual but familiar grin began to spread across his greasy face. It wasn't the look of a man caught in a moment of despair. It was the look of a man who had seemingly just recognized an old acquaintance. His grin widened, almost as if he found some twisted satisfaction in the fact that Foret was the one who had come to arrest him.

Baptiste froze for a split second, the unsettling recognition hitting her like a punch to the gut. She watched the way Breaux looked at Foret, the familiarity in his expression. It was the same look she had seen just a few days earlier, after the assault on their beloved Father Landry. She had seen that same look in Breaux's eyes—like he knew Pete, like they shared some history, some connection that ran deeper than just this case.

It hit her all at once, and her pulse quickened as the pieces of the puzzle clicked together. Yes, this was the guy, the same Mark Breaux that had graciously walked through their hectic crime scene at the church and made strange grinning eye contact with Pete. This guy was at the scene, only a few yards away from her, and he literally walked right past her. Her feelings that he was oddly too calm that day had now been realized. What had also just been realized was that there was something more to Pete's involvement in the case than meets the eye, and seeing Breaux's second reaction towards him confirmed her suspicions even more. *Pete had to know this guy. Could they have been past lovers? Pete wasn't gay, she knew that firsthand, but you never know about people's past. Could Pete be ashamed of their past relations, desperately trying to keep it under wraps?* There had to be a past here, one that she had yet to fully understand.

For a moment, everything seemed to slow down, and the weight of the situation shifted. They were going to be bringing this criminal to justice, but was this more personal than she had ever thought? Her gaze darted to Foret, searching for some hint, some explanation. But he wasn't looking at her—his eyes were intently fixed on Breaux, and his jaw was clenched so tightly it was a wonder his teeth didn't crack. The pressure in the room was immeasurable, and it wasn't just the impending arrest that made it so thick, it had to be the unspoken history between the two men.

Baptiste steeled herself. She couldn't afford to let her personal doubts and suspicions cloud her judgment at this stressful moment. This was an operation, and they had a job to do. But as she watched Foret and Breaux share that unnerving, knowing look, she realized that this definitely wasn't just another bust. Something much deeper was at play here, and she would have to dig into it later. Right now, they had their suspect to arrest.

Without taking his right hand out of his robe, Breaux says, "Well, well Mr. Foret. Sorry I didn't answer the door, but I was speaking to our Father. And you know as well as anyone, he waits for no man."

Pete quickly yells, "Take your hand out of your pocket now!"

Breaux replies, "Pete, just relax, I'm-"

Pete instantly unloads three or four shots out of his 9mm Beretta, directly into Breaux.

Baptiste yells, "Nooooo!"

She then pushes Pete and his pistol out of her way as she leaps to aid Breaux, his body sliding to the floor after flying backwards into the closest wall. A smeared blood trail became instantly noticeable on the wall and growing on the floor around the dying Breaux. As she bends down to attend to the wounded Vindicator, he grimaces while trying to smile. His momentary distracting body odor leaves her thoughts as she focuses on his hand slowly coming out of his pocket. Always alert, she focuses on his hand, making sure he has no weapons for one final and desperate attack. His hand continues to slowly rise to reveal a rosary and a tattered Bible. He offers both of the religious objects to her and painfully whispers while looking up to the ceiling, "Father, I have failed you, please have mercy."

As Mark Breaux's final breath rattled through his chest, his body gave a slight tremor, then settled entirely. His head, heavy with the weight of his demise, fell onto Baptiste's lap. She froze for a

## CHAPTER 10: THE NET CLOSES IN

moment, her heart pounding, staring down at the lifeless man. Her hands hovered over him in disbelief, hoping as though she could somehow reverse what had just happened. But there was no mistaking it. Mark Breaux, the man they had hunted for months, was dead, and Pete Foret was responsible. Baptiste's gaze lifted from Breaux's wide-open eyes and lifeless face towards Pete, who stood frozen inside the doorway, his smoking gun still in his hand, his expression unreadable. It was a moment of pure shock, and Baptiste couldn't help the rising wave of disgust and astonishment that bubbled to the surface. Her voice cracked as she spoke, a mix of confusion and anger. "What the hell was that, Pete?"

His eyes flickered with uncertainty, but his lips tightened into a line. He hesitated for a moment, then responded in an almost defensive tone. "What, I thought he was going for a weapon?"

The words left his mouth with an air of justification, but there was a tremor beneath his calm exterior, one Baptiste could see—an attempt to rationalize something that shouldn't have needed to be rationalized.

Baptiste shot to her feet, disappointment flooding her every muscle. She towered over Breaux's body for a moment, her eyes never leaving Pete as she fired back.

"What weapon, Pete? All he had was a Bible and a freakin' rosary!"

Her voice rose in frustration, the disbelief clear in every word. She had seen the rosary in Breaux's hand, and had seen the tattered Bible. Symbols of something she had never truly believed in but symbols all the same. There had been no weapon, no threat to her or anyone else in the room. Just a dying man clinging to some bizarre notion of redemption. She turned away from him, pushing past the weight of the moment. She tried to push down the sick feeling that churned in her stomach, but the image of his lifeless form—the mess of blood now staining the room—would haunt her for some time.

As she stood, her body trembling with anger, she marched past Pete as he tried to grab her by the arm, "Zoe."

She snatches her arm away from his feudal grasp, "No Pete, don't. That was a rookie move! You know better than that."

Just as another one of the team's officers enters the room with his sidearm drawn, he asks aloud, "Damn, what happen?"

As Zoe walks by the fellow deputy, she slyly responds, "Pistol Pete gets another one."

She storms out of the dark room, her footsteps quick and purposeful. Pete, his expression still unreadable, follows her out without hesitation.

"Alright Pete, you got his ass," the smiling deputy states while holding out his hand for a congratulatory fist bump.

Pete pushed him out of the way as he ignored his teammate's gesture and praise. His heart racing in his chest, the adrenaline coursing through his veins as the realization hit him hard, he had crossed a line. He had acted impulsively, without thinking. And now, it was too late to take it back. The implications of what he had just done were enormous. A man, dangerous, yet still a man, was dead, and Pete was the one who had pulled the trigger. The weight of that knowledge pressed down on him, and the walls seemed to close in on him as he followed Baptiste through the now crowded narrow hallway and out of the apartment.

Outside, the chaos of the scene unfolded around them. Officers were still securing the area, moving back and forth in calculated efficiency, each one oblivious to the tension between their two colleagues. Baptiste was a blur of motion as she bobbed and weaved through the crowd, her body language tight with disgust. Pete was right on her heels, pushing through the crowd of uniformed officers, trying to catch up with her. His mind raced, filled with the rush of guilt and fear as the adrenaline began to ebb and the reality of the situation set in.

When they were out of ear shot from the others, Pete took a breath, trying to steady himself. His voice was strained, the urgency in it unmistakable.

"Zoe, listen to me!"

He reached for her arm, but she pulled away sharply again, not meeting his eyes. "We can't let anyone know about what happened here. We need to get our stories straight, please."

She stopped walking, her body rigid. She turned to face him, her eyes filled with a mixture of anger and betrayal. For a long moment, she said nothing. The words burned on the tip of her tongue, and finally, she spat them out with raw emotion.

"What story, Pete?"

Her voice was ice cold now, a stark contrast to the rage that had been bubbling in her chest moments before.

"You think I can just cover up an unwarranted murder? Mark Breaux may have been dangerous, but you pulled the trigger this time! That wasn't the plan, and you know it! We were to capture him first for interrogation."

Pete's chest tightened at her words. He had acted too quickly, and now, standing before Baptiste, he couldn't deny the truth. He had killed Breaux. No matter what the justification, no matter the circumstances, Breaux was dead because of him. And Baptiste knew it.

He tried to steady his voice, his hands still trembling slightly as he spoke.

"Zoe, I— I really didn't have a choice. He was reaching for something. I thought he was going for a weapon. I couldn't take the risk."

His words felt hollow, as though he was trying to convince himself more than her.

Baptiste shook her head, her expression hardening. "You didn't have a choice?"

Her voice was low, but every syllable carried the weight of her disbelief.

"Pete, you didn't have to pull that trigger. He wasn't an immediate threat. You could've waited. We could've taken him in alive."

She took a step back, crossing her arms tightly in front of her chest. Her body language was closed off now, as if shutting him out entirely.

"But now we're here. And you're asking me to cover up a pointless killing. This man is dead because you panicked. We can't just pretend it didn't happen, Pete."

The words hung in the tension of the moment. Pete opened his mouth to respond, but the words wouldn't come. Zoe was right. She had every right to be angry, every right to feel let down. He had crossed a line, uncharted territory for them both. The realization that this wasn't just about a mistake made in the heat of the moment, it was about trust. This was about their partnership, their years of working together—faith that had been shattered in an instant. Pete's hands dropped to his sides, his heartrate speeding not from adrenaline anymore, but now, from fear. Fear of what would come next, fear of the fallout. He couldn't undo what he had done, and now neither of them could escape the consequences.

She turned away from him, her eyes hard and unforgiving.

"I need time to think," she muttered, her voice cold. "I don't

## CHAPTER 10: THE NET CLOSES IN

know if I can even look at you right now, Pete."

With that, she walked away, leaving him standing alone. The reality of his actions pressing down on him like a thousand-pound anchor. She didn't look back as she continued, her mind reeling, the bitter taste of betrayal lingering in her mouth.

The early-evening air began to set, and she unstrapped her bullet-proof vest as she moved toward their unmarked squad car, the world around her blurring. She needed to get out of there, away from the scene, away from the officers who might have seen something she hadn't. She needed space to breathe, to unwind and think.

But just as she reached her car, a voice cut through the air, sharp and insistent.

"Detective Baptiste, hold up!"

She didn't stop, her hand already on the door handle, but the voice was louder this time, more urgent.

"Detective, wait just a minute!"

She hesitated, but then turned slowly, her shoulders tense, her jaw clenched.

Standing several feet away was Lieutenant Rodriguez, a colleague she'd worked with before, along with a couple of others she recognized. They were all looking at her with a mix of expectation and wariness, their eyes darting between her and the chaos still unfolding outside of the apartment.

Rodriguez stepped forward; his hand raised in a placating gesture.

"Look, Zoe, first off, good job—and glad you're safe. Secondly, we're all just a bit confused, and we're trying to figure out what happened in there." His voice was a bit too calm, too controlled for her liking.

"We're gonna need an official statement you know. It's protocol, you know the drill."

Her heart pounded in her chest, and she could feel the anger rising again, a rush of heat flooding her face. She'd been there for hours, making sure every move was calculated and measured, and now, here they were asking her to explain the situation with the same detached professionalism that had started this whole nightmare.

"I'm not giving a statement right now," Baptiste snapped, the words sharp, her voice a low growl.

"Not tonight."

Rodriguez stepped closer, sensing her resistance but not backing down.

"We're just trying to understand why deadly force was necessary," he pressed, his tone more urgent now.

"I get it, Breaux was a dangerous guy, but we need to know why Pete fired. Was he going for a weapon, because we didn't find one? Did you feel threatened?"

His eyes flicked to her hand, which was still hovering near her car door, but he was watching her face now, searching for any sign of weakness. Her fingers curled into a fist. She didn't want to do this. She didn't want to stand there and explain what had happened in that room, not when she could barely process it herself. But there was no avoiding it. Rodriguez and the others weren't going to let her walk away.

She took a slow breath, trying to keep her composure.

"I don't know, okay? I don't know what Pete was thinking. I wasn't watching him, wasn't paying attention to his hand. I saw him shoot, and I saw Breaux fall."

Her voice was flat, disconnected, as though she were saying the words without truly understanding them herself.

Rodriguez gave a small nod, though it was clear he wasn't satisfied.

"But you were in the room when it happened. You were close enough to see what was going on, to know if there was any real threat." Rodriguez paused, his gaze hardening slightly.

"You're telling me you couldn't tell if Breaux was reaching for a weapon either?"

"I didn't see anything," Baptiste shot back, the words coming out quicker now, frustration boiling over.

"All I saw was him with a Bible and a rosary. I don't know what Pete saw. He's the one who pulled the trigger."

Her voice cracked slightly, despite her best efforts to remain calm. She felt the weight of the situation—the guilt, anger, the confusion—crushing her from all sides.

Rodriguez's gaze softened for just a moment, but it was fleeting.

"You know how it looks, right?" he said, his voice quieter, more serious.

"It looks almost like an execution, Zoe. One second, Breaux is praying or whatever the hell he was doing, and the next, he's dead. Pete fired without any real provocation." He shook his head, his expression hardening again.

"I don't care about what kind of history you two have, this is a serious situation."

Her hardened gaze flickered toward the other officers standing behind Rodriguez, their faces impassive. They were waiting for her to say something, anything that would clarify the situation, something that would make sense of what had truly happened inside. But nothing about this made sense. Not the way Breaux had died, not Pete's actions, and certainly not the way everything was unfolding now. In a matter of minutes, they had gone from eventual heroes to now being questionable cops.

"Pete probably panicked," she muttered under her breath, more to herself than to anyone else.

But Rodriguez heard her.

"What do you mean by that?" he asked, his eyes narrowing slightly.

"I mean he didn't think I guess," she responded, her voice growing tighter with each word.

"He felt he saw Breaux move, and he reacted. No hesitation, no second thought. He didn't wait to see if Breaux was reaching for something. He just shot. And now we have a very dangerous dead man on our hands and a whole mess to clean up, I guess. At least this nightmare is over, right?"

Rodriguez remained silent for a moment, weighing her words. He seemed to understand the gravity of her statement, but that didn't change the fact that they needed more definitive answers—answers that Baptiste wasn't ready to give. She knew that a man had died, and she knew that Pete's actions had escalated the situation to the point of no return. But she also knew something else—if she kept talking, if she kept explaining, it would all spiral even more out of control. She could feel the stress of the entire department bearing down on her.

"I'm done talking about this right now," the finality in her voice unmistakable.

She didn't wait for a response before she opened the door of her car and slid inside, slamming it shut behind her. The engine roared to life, and with a burst of power, she sped off into the night, leaving Rodriguez and the others standing in the dust.

Rodriguez stood there for a long moment, watching Baptiste's

## CHAPTER 10: THE NET CLOSES IN

car peel away into the evening, its taillights swallowed by the darkness. His mind unsettled as the tension of the scene settled into an uncomfortable silence. He didn't like where things were headed. Baptiste's reaction had been too quick, too raw. And Pete... well, Pete had acted without thinking, and now, the aftermath was going to be a hell of a lot more complicated than anyone had originally anticipated. Rodriguez let out a slow, controlled breath and turned on his heel, heading back toward the apartment building. As he moved, the clatter of other officers and the low hum of radio chatter filled the air, but everything felt distant, muted—like a bad dream he couldn't or wouldn't wake up from. It wasn't always pretty, but this was his job.

Back inside the apartment, the scene was still being processed. Officers were gathering evidence, taking photos, and securing the area. But none of them seemed to know what to say. The air was loaded with unspoken questions hanging above all of the additional team members. Rodriguez shook his head as he stepped through the door, a part of him wishing he could forget about the whole damn thing. But he couldn't.

Foret had returned and was standing in the hallway, his back against the wall, his arms crossed, staring down at the floor. The usual confident, sharp-eyed officer was nowhere to be seen. In his place was a man who looked as if the world had been yanked from under him, a man trying to come to terms with a decision that had crossed a line from law enforcement to something much darker. His 9mm was holstered, but his fingers still twitched as though the gun was an extension of himself, something he couldn't quite shake.

Rodriguez approached slowly, eyes concentrating on Pete's face, trying to gauge how much he had processed of what had just transpired. The sound of his footsteps on the hardwood floor seemed too loud in the tense silence.

"Pete," Rodriguez began, his voice measured but firm, "I need a statement man. We need to know what happened here. What led to the use of deadly force."

He paused, his tone a little softer now, "I need you to be totally honest with me."

Pete didn't immediately look up. His eyes remained focused on the floor, like he was searching for an answer that wasn't there. He opened his mouth to speak, but nothing came out at first. Then, in a strained voice, he muttered, "I thought he was reaching for a weapon, man. I don't know what else to tell you."

Rodriguez waited, giving him a couple of moments. But Pete didn't offer anything more, and Rodriguez could feel the stress sinking in. He couldn't shake the image of Breaux lying in a pool of blood with nothing but an openhand that held a Bible and rosary. It just didn't add up, it looked bad, and Rodriguez was starting to wonder if Pete was just trying to convince himself of something, and trying to convince everyone else.

"Pete," Rodriguez said again, this time quieter, "You've been in this game long enough to know that sometimes, in the heat of the moment, we make mistakes. But we're all watching you right now. I need you to think clearly. You need to tell me exactly what happened. No excuses."

He stepped closer, his eyes locked with Pete's.

"I need the truth."

Pete's jaw clenched. His knuckles whitened as his hands gripped the edge of the door frame, his eyes tightening.

"I told you.....I thought he was going to pull something, alright?" Pete snapped, his voice rising slightly, the weight of his actions

## CHAPTER 10: THE NET CLOSES IN

breaking through his calm facade.

"He was just sitting there, staring at me with that goddamn grin. I told him to take his hand out of his pocket, but he didn't listen. I wasn't gonna take a chance. I'm not that stupid."

His voice cracked slightly as he continued, "It was just a split-second decision. I saw the movement, and I pulled the trigger. I don't know what else you want me to say, Rodriguez."

The Lieutenant absorbed the words, watching the emotions flicker in Pete's eyes—regret maybe, or fear. But there was something else in there too, something that told Rodriguez this wasn't just about a mistake, he was too good of a cop. This was about something deeper, possibly something personal. He could tell Pete wasn't entirely convinced by his own explanation. His voice trembled, betraying a crack in the tough exterior Pete usually wore.

Rodriguez remained silent for a moment, considering. Then he took another deep breath, lowering his voice.

"Look, Pete, I know you've been through a lot. And I know Breaux was dangerous. But we—" he gestured toward the officers working the scene, "—we need to know that you followed protocol. You know the rules. You know what deadly force requires. And from where I'm standing, it looks like you acted on impulse."

Pete's eyes flicked up to meet Rodriguez's, and for the first time, Rodriguez saw a flash of something that looked like shame. It was gone almost instantly, but it was there, another brief crack in the façade.

"Yeah, I acted on impulse. I'll admit that" Pete muttered, the words coming out more bitter than he probably intended.

"But I'm not going to apologize for protecting myself. You weren't there. You didn't see him, how he was looking at me. You didn't hear what he said to me. The man was insane."

Rodriguez was silent for a long moment, watching Pete. It was hard to deny the truth in his words. Breaux had been unpredictable, violent, and they all knew how much danger he posed. But even so, Rodriguez couldn't shake the nagging feeling that something just wasn't right. Something about how Pete had reacted, it was more than just fear.

Rodriguez started, his tone softer now.

"Well, we're gonna have to do an internal review, you know that, right? You've got a solid history, but this… this doesn't just go away."

Pete's gaze hardened, his jaw tightening.

"I get it," he said, his voice flat. "I did what I had to do."

He stepped away from the door frame, his back straightened, like he was preparing himself for what came next.

Rodriguez nodded, giving Pete one last look before turning to head back toward the door. He had what he needed for now, but there were no doubt things were about to get a lot messier. The internal review, the investigation—it would all come down to what everyone involved said happened in that room. And right now, the story was fractured, full of holes. This wasn't over, not by a long shot.

# CHAPTER 11: AFTERMATH

Baptiste had spent the last few days piecing together fragments of evidence that seemed to slip through the cracks of her partner's narratives. Pete had always been a reliable ally, a steadfast figure in her life who had guided her through the murky waters of police work with a steady hand. They had shared countless hours of productive investigation, each successful case a testament to their effective teamwork. But after the unfortunate incident with the unarmed Mark Breaux, everything felt tainted, like a once-vibrant painting smeared with a dark brushstroke. The scene replayed in her mind: Breaux, non-confrontational and calm, Foret, gun drawn, his expression a mixture of resolve and something darker. The suspect had posed no apparent or immediate threat, and yet his life was snuffed out in a heartbeat. Foret was too quick and deliberate, like it was a predetermined and forgone conclusion in his mind.

Breaux, the doomed suspect, had stood there, non-aggressive and calm, his hands visibly empty, yet somehow Foret had perceived a threat that wasn't truly there. Baptiste could still see the way Foret had moved, his gun drawn with a fluidity that suggested his actions were a rehearsed maneuver, practiced and ingrained. His expression had been a mixture of determination and something slightly sinister, an intensity that had been etched in her memory. In that fleeting moment, the world had narrowed down to the two of them—Foret and Breaux—while everything else faded into the background. The gunshots had echoed in her ears long after the silence returned, a haunting reminder that life could be extinguished in an instant. And now she felt that she knew why. The same odd feeling she had suspected even before that fateful day. There had to be some sort of prior knowledge between the two. Breaux had to know Pete, and he was going to extinguish their apparent familiarity quickly.

She poured a glass of red wine, its deep crimson hue swirling in the glass, mirroring the tumult of emotions churning within her. Each sip should have offered a moment of solace, but instead, it only heightened her awareness of the implications of what she felt she had uncovered. After late nights spent hunching over her desk, sifting through reports and interred case files, Baptiste had stumbled upon a troubling trail that led her deeper into a labyrinth of deceit. The more she discovered, the more her heart sank, caught in a relentless tug-of-war between loyalty to her partner and her commitment to justice. Her mind rushed as she rehashed the events immediately following Foret's fatal encounter with Breaux. She recalled the frantic moments in the aftermath, the chaos of the agitated crime scene, the gathering crowd of curious onlookers, their expressions, a mixture of relief, disbelief, and horror. It all continues to replay in her mind as she sits alone for now, her heart melancholy in the wake of Foret's imposed departure. He has been placed on temporary leave while internal affairs conducts their in-

## CHAPTER 11: AFTERMATH

vestigation. But unbeknownst to them all, Zoe was doing her own investigation as well. The air felt dense with unspoken truths, each moment stretching into a taut silence that echoed with the weight of her thoughts. She could almost hear the unvoiced accusations hovering in the corners of the room, pressing against her like a physical force. But one truth stood out more clearly than the rest: she had to know everything, and she would.

Determined, she grabbed her jacket from the hook by the door, the fabric brushing against her skin like a cloak of resolve. As she stepped out into the night, the cool air hit her face, sharpening her drained senses. The streetlights cast long shadows on the pavement, their flickering glow illuminating her path as she followed one of the routes Breaux had taken to commit one of the many assaults he had orchestrated. Each step felt heavy with purpose, her heels echoing in the strange, but now safe stillness around her.

She had a hunch, a nagging suspicion that Mark Breaux might not have been the only one involved at the center of it all. *Could he have pulled off such a large number of attacks around the whole city by himself?* They recently had found out that the man didn't even own a car. He had to have had some type of help. She always kind of felt at the back of her mind that it may be more than one person involved. They just never could prove it. Just the fact that he was so hard to catch, and the amount of ground he seemed to cover without being seen, it was just too complicated for him to pull off alone, and for so long.

Even now, his death had felt too clean, too calculated. He was an unarmed suspect caught in the crosshairs of a strange, yet tense moment. The more she thought about it, the more it gnawed at her, like a puzzle with a missing piece that refused to fit anywhere else. The scenario played over in her mind, scenes replaying with vivid clarity, the look in Breaux's eyes, the smirk of familiarity shown to Pete, the way he had basically surrendered, the flash of Foret's weapon. It all seemed too orchestrated, too convenient to be just an unfortunate accident.

As she continued through the now quiet streets, the city felt different, cloaked in an unsettling aura that mirrored her turmoil. The terror was over, but there still was something bothering her. The shadows seemed to whisper secrets, and every rustle of leaves made her pulse quicken. She recalled the faces of those who had witnessed the encounter, the flicker of fear and disbelief etched in their expressions. She felt an urgency to connect the dots before they slipped away, the fragments of evidence and intuition swirling in her mind like a storm threatening to break.

The next day, Baptiste arrived at the precinct, the atmosphere was somewhat subdued as the dim lights flickered above the offices. Officers were wrapping up their shifts, their faces a bit weary from the weight of a day spent navigating the murky waters of crime and justice. Even though the department was grateful that the Vindicator had been extinguished, the city would always have criminals to defend the innocent from. She greeted a few colleagues absentmindedly, her mind already racing with the task ahead. The precinct felt like a web of secrets, and she was determined to unravel one of its darkest threads: What was the deal with Pete and Breaux, and why was it still bothering her?

She settled into her desk, pushing aside various case files and paperwork, her fingers deftly rifling through the chaos in search of any mention of Mark Breaux. Hours ticked away, the clock on the wall echoing her mounting frustration. The rhythmic ticking grew louder, a methodic passage of time, as she sifted through the endless stacks of reports, some mundane, others more chilling. Her

## CHAPTER 11: AFTERMATH

resolve remained unshaken; she knew that Breaux's connections were crucial to understanding the larger picture.

As the night lengthened and the precinct began to empty, she finally stumbled upon a concealed confidential report on Pete's desk, hidden beneath a pile of routine files. The words leapt out at her, grim and foreboding. Breaux had been implicated as a possible suspect in some of the attacks by some of his neighbors, but it was the last line that sent a chill racing down her spine. Breaux should have been under investigation for multiple charges, but alarmingly, evidence suggested that his name had been covered up and removed by someone within the department itself. It was Pete!

"Damn it," she whispered, realization crashing over her like a tidal wave.

Foret had not only shot Breaux; he had manipulated the entire case file on Breaux, all while maintaining the facade of a loyal detective. *But why would he do this?* As she dug deeper into the implications, the answer twisted in her gut. This was not merely about greed or ambition; it was rooted in something darker, something profoundly disturbing. Foret's actions seemed to be driven by the same warped sense of justice that Breaux had operated with. His need to punish, and Breaux's wish to punish by teaching and to save.

She wandered over to the personnel files room to carefully dig into Pete's history. The deeper she delved into his files, the more unsettling the truth became. She unearthed details about Pete's past—his brief, troubled stint in seminary school. Expelled for his harsh interpretations of scripture, he had been cast out for his radical beliefs, along with being romantically linked to one of the nuns employed at the school. The notion of "an eye for an eye" had been a rallying cry for him, a doctrine he had taken to heart with dangerous fervor. The more she read, the more horrifying it became. It was clear that Foret had simply not wanted to just uphold the law; he desired to be its executioner, a twisted savior cleansing the world of what he perceived as sin. And Breaux was the perfect fanatical zealot to help him with his supremely unorthodox plan for the city's sinners. What he couldn't accomplish with the department's resources, he would have done with his old acquaintance, Breaux.

Thinking back on her time with Pete as her partner, he was always the detective with the least amount of patience. But she never suspected anything like this, he had covered up his true feelings quite well. *What had been said? Had Foret been baiting him, luring him into a trap?* The unsettling thoughts lingered, adding even more weight to her growing conviction.

As the days turned into a blur of late nights and early mornings, Zoe's focus sharpened. Each piece of evidence she gathered painted a more intricate portrait of Foret—a great actor who had been warped by his own beliefs. He was bitter from his past and had grown to appreciate his love of power, a power he would not relinquish easily.

After passing on this information to Father Landry, he was also greatly surprised at what she was relaying. Landry was now her only true partner, and after praying with her, agreed that Pete needed to be exposed. She needed the priest to be aware of what she had found, just in case she was not successful in persuading Pete to giving himself up, or if she was killed during the process. Landry, always a soldier of the truth, stood confident by Baptiste in her decision. He knew this time was difficult but reminded her that the Lord would smile down on her with his protection. She considered not telling her mother during a last visit before contacting Pete, but she decided to let her know. She felt Zumaya deserved to know after all the advice she had given her throughout the long investigation. Zoe was also glad that she got to at least see her mama once more, just in case she didn't survive the soon-to-be-planned meeting with her disgraced partner. She began to formulate a strategy, knowing that the intimidating confrontation was inevitable. But she needed to approach it with caution, understanding that Foret was not just a colleague; he was a man who saw the world in black and white, with no room for shades of gray. She couldn't help but think to herself once again, *had his feelings for her been fake as well?*

The warm glow of the dining room lamp illuminated the table, casting flickering shades against the walls. Zoe meticulously arranged the plates, each detail, a distraction from the storm brewing in her mind. The rich aroma of the simmering pot of roux wafted through the air, leaving her appetite for a warm bowl of gumbo to be overshadowed by the anticipation of her guest's arrival. As she placed the last spoon down, she glanced at the clock, its ticking echoing like a metronome, keeping time with her racing thoughts. Each tick seemed to amplify the weight of her decision to confront Foret. She had spent years guarding her privacy, especially in her own home, but she felt this private setting was the right place to talk with Pete.

The dining room, with its wooden table and mismatched chairs, felt more intimate than ever, yet it also seemed to harbor secrets. The warmth of the lamp created a cocoon of light that contrasted with the encroaching shadows, inviting yet enigmatic. Old family photographs adorned the walls, each frame a silent witness to the gatherings and conversations that had taken place here over the years. There were images of laughter-filled holidays, where the clinking of glasses mingled with the sound of cheerful voices, and others depicting solemn moments, where shared glances spoke volumes amid the weight of loss. These snapshots served as reminders of joy and sorrow, love and heartache. Elements of her past that now felt intertwined with the tension of the growing moment.

As her eyes wandered over the frames, she caught glimpses of her childhood self, wide-eyed and innocent, flanked by relatives whose faces held a tapestry of stories. Her grandmother's gentle smile radiated warmth, a stark contrast to the resolve that now defined her life. She recalled how the dining room had been a shelter—a place where familial bonds were forged over shared meals and laughter, yet it also bore the marks of unspoken conflicts and unresolved issues.

As she stirred the pot, the Cajun roux thickening to a deep, rich color, she allowed herself a moment to breathe. The smell of smoked sausage mingled with the spices—paprika, cayenne, and thyme—creating an intoxicating aroma that filled the room and wrapped around her like a warm embrace. It reminded Zoe of her grandmother's kitchen, where laughter and stories flowed as freely as the gumbo itself, blending into a vibrant family history. She could almost hear her grandmother's voice, rich and melodic, recounting tales of old, punctuated by the sound of pots clanging and the soft hum of a well-loved tune playing in the background.

But that comfort felt distant now, overshadowed by the weight of what was to come. The warmth of nostalgia was tempered by a gnawing anxiety that settled in her stomach like a stone. She wondered if her guest would be able to take the accusations calmly or if he would erupt into confrontation, shattering the peace and comradery they had crafted these last few years. They had no

## CHAPTER 11: AFTERMATH

contact since his suspension went into effect, so this was going to be an awkward interaction at best. The thought sent a quiver of uneasiness down her back. She had seen enough turmoil in her career to know how quickly a situation could escalate.

As she continued to stir, her thoughts spiraled into possibilities, each scenario darker than the last. *Would her guest react defensively, casting doubt on her instincts? Or would Pete acknowledge the truth she was desperate to uncover?* The prospect of conflict loomed large, threatening to turn her carefully prepared meal into a battlefield. She recalled moments from her past where honesty had cost her dearly, times when the truth had felt like a double-edged sword, cutting through relationships and trust.

The doorbell chimed, jolting her from her thoughts. Taking a deep breath, she composed herself and opened the door. Pete stood on the threshold, his expression as warm as the evening light.

"Zoe! Smells amazing in here," stepping inside, his smile genuine yet somehow too polished.

"Thanks, I thought we could use a little normalcy," gesturing for him to take a seat at the table.

The familiar banter they shared felt strained now, heavy with unspoken truths. They settled in, the conversation drifting to mundane topics—cases they'd solved, old colleagues, plans for the weekend. But Baptiste could feel the tension creeping in, an undercurrent of anxiety that made the air feel thick.

"Zoe, you seem a little off tonight," concern etched on his face. "Everything okay?"

She took a sip of her merlot, gathering her thoughts quickly.

"Actually, there is something I need to talk to you about."

"Sure, what's on your mind, Zoe?" leaning forward slightly, his demeanor shifting from casual to attentive.

She cleared her throat, heart pounding.

"It's about the shooting, Pete. And it's about the whole damn case. I've been doing some digging, and... I'm worried about what I've found."

Foret's brow furrowed, and an eclipse appeared in his eyes.

"What do you mean?"

She took a deep breath, trying to steady her speeding heart. The atmosphere in the dining room felt charged, the soft clinking of silverware now fading away. She leaned in closer, lowering her voice.

"It's about Breaux," she began, her tone cautious.

"I know he had connections to some pretty dark places, but the more I uncovered, the more it seemed like he was being manipulated. I can't help but think you played a role in that. My suspicions were right, you did know him."

His expression tightened, his features becoming more guarded.

"What are you implying Zoe?" he asked, a hint of defensiveness creeping into his voice.

"Mark was under investigation for multiple crimes, but evidence suggests you orchestrated covering for him multiple times, and I even saw you speaking with him on one of the traffic cameras the same day of the sting."

She pressed on, her resolve hardening.

"You shot him, Pete. To silence him. To keep your own name clean."

His eyes narrowed once more, and he leaned back in his chair, crossing his arms defensively.

"You're jumping to conclusions, Zoe. You don't have all the facts. Mark was the Vindicator, a loose cannon; he was dangerous."

"But you didn't just shoot a dangerous man," she countered, her

## CHAPTER 11: AFTERMATH

voice steady despite the tension.

"You set him up. You used him and turned him into your scapegoat, and then silenced him. All those religious crimes—Breaux was the one doing the damage and ready to take the fall, but you were the one pulling the strings."

"Don't be naive," Foret snapped, his voice low and intense.

"You think I wanted to kill him? I had no choice. It was him or me. He was too deep in it, and he was going to blow the whole operation."

"Operation?" Baptiste echoed, her stomach twisting.

"What operation? This isn't just about Breaux. This is about you playing God, thinking you're some kind of righteous judge. I know you were expelled from the same seminary too. Was that where you learned this twisted sense of justice, or were you always going to be vindictive because you were asked to leave?"

His gaze hardened into almost a scowl, and he leaned forward even more, his voice a harsh whisper.

"You don't understand the world we live in, Zoe. People like Breaux deserve punishment. He served his purpose for the Lord, and for me, he was just getting out of hand. I was only doing what needed to be done to cleanse the rot. You of all people know the system is corrupt. We arrest the criminals and a week later they are back on the streets, often even sooner."

"Cleanse the rot?" she repeated, incredulous.

"By maiming people and then murdering Breaux? You're not a savior, Pete. You're a monster hiding behind a badge, using your position to manipulate and destroy lives."

He flinched at her words, but his expression remained defiant.

"I'm doing what the system fails to do. Aren't you sick of criminals getting off with a slap on the wrist, or worse yet, getting away totally? You're too idealistic, Zoe. You think justice can be served in neat little packages, but the reality is much messier."

"Messier?" Baptiste shot back.

"You've crossed a line that can't be undone. You think you're above the law because you wear that badge, but you're just as guilty as those you claim to hunt down. This isn't justice; it's vengeance, and you've let it consume you. Even Breaux did what he did thinking he was helping them in the long run."

For a moment, silence hung between them, dense with unspoken truths. She watched as a flicker of uncertainty crossed Foret's face, quickly masked by his steely demeanor.

"You need to stop this," he warned, his tone low and threatening. "You're walking a dangerous path, Baptiste. If you push this, you'll regret it."

She felt her heart beginning to beat even faster, but she stood her ground.

"Regret? I'd rather face whatever comes than turn a blind eye to what you've done. You can't keep hiding behind your so-called righteous mission. I will expose the truth, even if it means taking you down with it."

His eyes blazed with a mix of anger and something akin to admiration.

"You've got guts, I'll give you that, you always did. But you're naive to think you can win this battle. I've been in this game longer than you realize, and I have friends who'll back me up. You'll be the one left standing alone in the end."

"I'd rather be alone and truthful than surrounded by lies," Baptiste retorted.

"You might think you have allies, but the walls are closing in. I'm not the only one starting to connect the dots. You can't keep your

## CHAPTER 11: AFTERMATH

actions hidden forever, Pete. This must end!"

With a measured breath, she leaned back, feeling the weight of her words settle on his face. His expression flickered, now a mixture of frustration and of slight fear, as he regarded her.

"Just know this, Baptiste," he said, his voice low and dangerous. "I've loved you, but once you cross me, there's no going back. Even after all that we've been through, I will still do whatever it takes to protect myself. You think you're the hero in this story, but the heroes fall. I'm also serving the Lord. I'm the true hero, but you can still join me!"

Her response was steady.

"I won't be intimidated into silence. True justice needs to be served, not your perverted justice, and I'm going to make sure it happens, even if it means exposing you, my oldest and closest ally. You are truly disappointing, Pete."

His gaze darkened, and for a brief moment, the air crackled with unspoken pressure, the line between predator and prey blurred in the flickering candlelight. In one instance, Foret was out of his seat and lunging at Baptiste. Both hands with an immediate grasp on the neck he once kissed and stroked with caress. Baptiste moans as her head is slammed on the table, and Foret just grunts as he continues to apply more pressure. She quickly rolls over the table in his direction, breaking the hold on her neck. She scrambles to her feet and swiftly knees him in the groin, allowing her to quickly break away. Gasping for air, she struggles to regain her breath and begins to hastily walk away from Foret and towards the couch to grab her sidearm resting on the small coffee table.

"You made a big mistake, Zoe" he snarled, his voice now a low growl.

Baptiste, startled but not unprepared, scrambled backwards,

her heart pounding wildly in her chest. She had pushed him too far, but she was also ready.

"You think you can just walk away from me, from us?"

Foret advanced, his hidden pistol steady.

"You think you can just expose me without consequences?"

"I'm not afraid of you," she replied dialed in and pointing her pistol at him, her voice steady despite the fear that gnawed at her. Her fingers gripped around the cold metal of her gun, gently shaking in her extended grasp.

After a long, tense few moments of their standoff, Foret reaches for this pistol, as Baptiste warns against this action. Foret continues and Baptiste fires her pistol just as he brings his up to also fire. They are both hit, and each of them instantaneously fall back from the close-range impact of each strike.

Foret is hit in his hand and drops his backup pistol to the floor. Baptiste is hit simultaneously in the leg and falls back onto the couch...the coach they once slept on.

Pete lunges to her and reaches to grab her with his bloody hands. But she was able to recover quicker than he expected. She rolls to the side, avoiding his grasp, and draws her weapon again.

Grimacing from the pain, she warns, "Don't move," her voice trembling slightly. "Don't make me do it, Pete!"

He froze, his eyes wide with surprise. He had underestimated her, and he knew better than anyone that he shouldn't have. *How could the woman he loved and worked with these last few years be doing this to him?* "Zoe, put down the gun baby," he demanded, his voice laced with uncertainty. While grimacing in pain, "Let's talk this shit out."

"Talk about what?" she answered, her finger tightening on the trigger. "There's nothing else to talk about. You've already done enough damage to the church, and to this entire city. You need to be exposed."

Another tense silence filled the room. The only sound was the soft ticking of the clock. Foret purposely hesitated. "You're bluffing," he said, his voice barely whispering. "After all that we've been through?"

"That's right, after all that we've been through." Baptiste replied, her voice unwavering.

"I feel like an idiot! My own partner betraying me and the city right under my nose. I would've brought you in a long time ago, but I knew you wouldn't have seen our way of thinking."

His eyes darted around the room, searching for an escape. But there was nowhere to run, nowhere to hide. He was trapped. "Let's just end this," his voice resigned. "We can both walk away from this."

"Not until you're behind bars," she counters. "You've hurt far too many people. You can't keep getting away with this."

He begins slowly inching toward her while continually trying to lure her into a false sense of security.

"Stop it Pete, don't make me do it!"

"Well, I'd rather die than live without having you as my partner ever again, I love you, Zoe!"

For a split second, their good times flashed through her memory, momentarily giving him the opening Foret felt he needed. His face instantly contorts into a mask of rage, and he lunges forward, but she is ready, as she always is. She fired once again, the shot echoing through the house. Foret stumbled backward, his bloody hand clutching his now wounded chest. He fell to the ground with a loud thump, his life already slipping away.

Baptiste stood over him, her breath ragged. She bent down, gingerly dropping to her knees, and squinting in pain. She grabs hold of his hand as he slyly grinned like he had so many times to her in the past. She reaches for her cell phone to call the ambulance, but he shakes his head.

"Don't bother, please."

She stops dialing and drops the phone on the floor, granting him his final wish.

After he expired, she closed both of his eyes, then wiped a few tears from her own eyes. She had done it, she had survived. But the victory was bittersweet. She had taken a life, the life of her best friend and partner, and that would haunt her forever. As she looked over his lifeless body, her hand was still trembling as she called for her fellow first responders. The echoes of the gunshot seemed to linger in the air, while her ear still was ringing from the close-range shots. It was a stark reminder of the violence that had just unfolded. Her heart pounded in her chest, a mixture of horror, relief and sorrow. She had survived, but at what cost?

As the adrenaline began to fade, a wave of nausea washed over her, her vision blurring. She had never imagined herself capable of such controlled violence. She had always been the one to preach peace and understanding, when possible, to turn the other cheek. But Foret had pushed her to her limit. He had forced her hand, just as he had guided and forced Breaux's hand as well.

The sound of sirens wailing in the distance jolted her back to reality. She knew the department would be there soon. She took a deep breath, readying herself. She had to face the consequences of her actions. She couldn't run away from them. *Would the department's reputation be tarnished even more after the news of Pete's treachery was made known to the media and the public?* The same public who was still healing from the torment of the Vindicator would now have the fresh wounds re-opened when they are made aware of this new twist to the epic story. Would they ever truly trust the police department again?

As the first responders eventually arrived, Baptiste remained seated on the floor, her gaze fixed on Foret's lifeless body. She watched as the paramedics worked tirelessly to revive him, but it was clear that he was gone. The police officers approached her cautiously to find out what had happened, their expressions a mix of concern and suspicion.

"Baptiste, are you alright? Can you tell us what happened here?" one of them asked, his voice cautious and steady.

She nodded, her voice barely a whisper.

"I'll live". Then nodding to Pete's body, "He was going to kill me, and I had to defend myself."

The officer responded astonished, "Pete was going to kill you?"

She hesitated, her mind racing, and still in shock. She knew she had to be careful. Revealing too much could jeopardize her safety and the safety of others. But she also knew that the truth had to come out.

"It's not just about Pete trying to kill me," she began, her voice crackling some. "Pete was a dangerous man. He's been manipulating these recent crimes and using them for his own twisted agenda. He was the one behind Mark Breaux's crimes."

The police officers exchanged astonished glances as their interest was piqued.

"Can you elaborate on that?" one of them asked.

Baptiste took a deep breath. "I was investigating the Mark Breaux case even after we got him. I started uncovering a pattern, a connection between his crimes and Foret. It all led back to Pete. He was the mastermind, pulling the strings, making sure Breaux took the fall if needed. Together they held our city hostage as they planned to cleanse our streets."

"How do you know this?" the officer pressed.

"I have evidence," Baptiste replied, her voice gaining strength. "I have a recorder on right now inside that cabinet, so you can hear for yourself, and I've been gathering a lot of hidden information, piecing together the puzzle. Don't worry, I have it all. I confronted Pete and he tried to kill me when I wouldn't stay quiet. He was a dangerous man, and he needed to be stopped."

The officers exchanged another look, their faces etched with even more surprised skepticism. But they could see the determination in her eyes, the fear and the resolve. They knew they had to take her seriously.

"We'll look into it. We can tackle this when you are better. But for now, we need to get you patched up. That leg of yours needs attention. You've been through a lot. Let's get you to the hospital."

Baptiste nodded; her eyes filled with fresh tears. She knew that the fight was far from over. But she was ready, ready to reveal the truth, no matter what the cost.